TWINK

TAYLOR SARACEN

TWINK

The Rise Up Series
Book Two
by
Taylor Saracen

13 Red Media Ltd.

PUBLISHER'S NOTE: This is a work of fiction. Names, characters, businesses, places, events, locales, and incidents are either the products of the author's imagination or used in a fictitious manner. Any resemblance to actual persons, living or dead, or actual events is purely coincidental.

TWINK

To Kyle

None of this would be possible without you. May your life be full of the joy you bring to everyone who knows you. My silly, sweet, smart friend, this book is for you.

ACKNOWLEDGMENTS

First and foremost, a big thank you to Keith Miller for understanding and enhancing the vision of this series. I'm perpetually impressed by his foresight and acuity. A special thank you to Kyle Ross for his continued support—on and off this project. It's been a privilege to work with him. An awed thank you to Emily Irwin for her ability to continuously create art that is more beautiful than I could have imagined. Thank you to Jill Savoia for being my go-to in all areas of everything, for her honesty, and most importantly, for her editing prowess. To Jenifer Friedman for opening my eyes to a world of possibility. Thank you to Michael Shulman for his mentorship and guidance. Finally, a resounding thank you to my family for their endless love and support in all I do.

ACKNOWLEDGMENTS

[illegible]

TWINK

1

There was only so much a body could endure and Kyle's had taken enough. Every time his thin frame was pushed against a row of lockers by relentless rednecks, he felt it for days. Black and blue welts blossomed on Texas-tanned skin, a reminder of what an outcast he was in the backwoods of Tennessee. They didn't want to understand him and he didn't expect them to try. Instead, he squeezed his eyes shut and braced for impact, never growing used to the pain, only learning to handle it. He'd dealt with worse. So had his car. It reverberated in his bones when the licorice-black paint of his Corvette was keyed by jealous jocks who didn't think a twink like him deserved such a masculine muscle car. They probably expected him to have a flaccid Ford Focus or something equally as impotent. It was unsettling to the hicks that he had more than them, had things they coveted.

Instinctively, Kyle held his breath as a sweaty ham hock hand clenched the nape of his neck and slammed his head into the door of girls' bathroom.

"This is where you piss from now on," the meathead growled, shoving Kyle into the lavatory. The cool tile floor chilled his beet-red cheeks as he lay on the ground, holding his knees close to his chest, hoping to avoid another hit. "Faggot."

The sound of the lock catching sent a rush of relief through his battered body. It was over—at least for the day.

"What the fuck?" a girl shrieked, falling to her knees next to Kyle. "Are you okay?"

He cringed when she touched his shoulder, exhausted by uninvited contact.

"Sorry," she muttered. "You're bleeding."

Kyle bristled and pulled himself to his feet. He wasn't a pussy. He didn't need to be cared for by some random cheerleader looking to do a good deed. "I'm fine."

Stumbling toward the sink, he steadied himself and turned on the faucet. A quick glance in the mirror confirmed that he was bleeding. Perhaps it wasn't as bad as it looked since noses bled a lot, broken or not. Shit, he hoped it wasn't broken. He was too pretty to risk a fucked-up mug.

Handful after handful of warm water washed away the evidence of the idiot's hatred as Kyle focused on his own. Faggot. That piece of shit had called him a faggot. Not only was the word reprehensible, but the implication that he was gay was irritating.

"Why are you in the ladies' room, creep?" a girl from Kyle's physics class asked as she exited a stall. The scowl on her face was as nasty as the tone of her voice.

"What's the difference?" he retorted, sweeping his blond locks off his forehead and glaring back at her. "I had to take a shit, and these toilets are way cleaner."

"You're disgusting," she scoffed, gaping at Kyle like he had four heads.

Deciding it wasn't worth engaging any further, Kyle dried his hands with a wad of paper towels, purposely cutting in front of her as he made his way to the trash can. She was worth irritating and he was eager to push her buttons. He'd been pushed enough; there was no reason not to push back.

"Rude," she huffed as Kyle crossed between her and the sink one more time.

She didn't know anything about rude. In the grand scheme of her life, Kyle was a gnat, an insignificant moment in time where she got more aggravated than she was at her boring baseline. True rudeness left an impact, and he was sure he would never register on her radar again. She'd bitch about Kyle's behavior to her friends over lunch, and he'd be forgotten by fifth period. How lucky she was to have the time and ability to worry about shit that didn't matter, while he was forced to focus on an endless succession of rude behavior that most certainly had changed the trajectory of his life. His mother's rampant selfishness had uprooted their lives, and she hadn't flinched. She put herself and her needs first, without so much as a thought about how it would affect her kids. *That* was rude.

Steeling himself for the next round of harassment, Kyle crossed his arms over his narrow chest before walking out of the bathroom and into the war zone. As expected, the bully who had been fucking with him moments before was directly across from the bathroom door, posted up against the lockers.

"You thought you could get away?" the bully snarled, cracking his knuckles as he walked toward Kyle.

Though Kyle wasn't sure how his panicked brain gave them the signal, his feet began to pick up speed, running away from the asshole, who was accelerating to catch him. The sound of sneakers squeaking against the tile floor filled the air, along with gasps and chuckles from the peers Kyle was shoving out of his way as he tried to escape the abuse. Stumbling over a girl who was squatting to tie her shoe, Kyle's back hit the ground. Attempting to crabwalk away from the encroaching bully, Kyle went wide-eyed as the bigger boy leaned in to lift his trembling body by the armpits. As his body was thrown against yet another row of lockers, Kyle stopped trying to get away. He was worn out from the initial beating and the chase and didn't have the wherewithal to fight anymore.

As if things couldn't get any worse, Kyle's crush—and Iris Valley High School's insanely handsome quarterback—Luke Larson was rushing toward them with fury flaming in his green eyes. It was bad enough to be bullied, but having a guy he drooled over join in was a new level of disheartening. To Kyle's surprise, Luke grabbed the bully by the neck and slammed him down to the ground. Relief washed over Kyle, making his tired body more wobbly than it had been moments before.

"Holy shit," Kyle muttered, glancing around at the group of students who had gathered around the scene. They'd probably think Luke was gay for standing up for him, and the boy-on-boy blemish on his reputation would get him run off the football team. Maybe then Luke would hate Kyle too.

"You don't touch him again," Luke seethed through gritted teeth. "Do you understand me?"

The bully quickly nodded his affirmation as a growing crowd watched the altercation with their jaws resting on the scuffed floor.

Kyle had never spoken to Luke save an occasional 'hey' when they passed each other in the hallway between sixth and seventh period. The football player had acknowledged Kyle maybe ten times, and Kyle had jacked off to the attention approximately ten thousand times. It was unfathomable that a guy like Luke was standing up for him in such a chivalrous way. And yet, he was.

After a couple more warnings, the quarterback let go of the bully and watched him as he scurried down the hallway. Once he was out of sight, Luke turned to regard Kyle.

"Are you alright?" he asked, moving closer to Kyle, who was frozen in place.

"I'm fine," Kyle replied, shoving his hands in the pockets of his skinny jeans.

Luke was so tall, handsome, and built, and it was intimidating for Kyle in the best possible way.

"I'm sorry you had to deal with that," Luke said softly, resting his hand tenderly on Kyle's cheek.

The touch made it difficult for Kyle to breathe. It was too much and not enough at the same time.

"I'm used to it," Kyle stated, chiding himself after the words escaped. He wasn't a victim. He didn't want Luke to think that was how he saw himself. "It's whatever."

"It's unacceptable," Luke corrected, leaning down to lay a passionate kiss on his lips.

It didn't feel real. Luke Larson was standing in the middle of IVHS's hallway making out with him. Somewhere in the back of his head, Kyle feared the affection was a part of a greater humiliation scheme, one that would hurt worse than the physical pounding he'd taken from the bushland bully. Despite his worries, the kiss was anything but disingenuous, pulsing with the passion of months of unrequited want.

"I'll be okay," Kyle promised, but the warble in his voice and wobbling of his knees indicated he was anything but. It was all too much, and suddenly he was exhausted by the goings-on.

Somehow, Luke understood his need for care and scooped him up in his gym-toned arms. The jaws that had already been on the floor were tugged down to the school's foundation and into the Earth below, burrowing beside the worries Kyle had finally been able to bury there, unnecessary concerns now that he'd found someone to protect him.

Tucking his face into the curve of Luke's neck, Kyle inhaled his savior's scent, letting the faint smell of sweat permeate his nostrils. And suddenly he was wet. Strains of saliva trickled from his mouth as his jeans struggled to contain the leaking hard-on pressing against them.

"Mr. Ross...Mr. Ross...MR. ROSS," a voice demanded, pummeling the perfect moment.

Kyle lifted his head and glanced around, startled by the sight of his peers sitting in desks rather than frozen in awe of Luke's display of heroism.

"What have I told you about sleeping in class?" his physics teacher, Mr. Meyer, asked, hands on his wide hips.

"Not to do it," Kyle offered, wiping his sleep-sloppy mouth with the back of his hand. He'd completely passed out.

"Don't sass me," Mr. Meyer warned.

"You asked me a question and I answered," Kyle sighed. "How is that sass?"

The older man regarded him for a beat. "I asked you a question. According to the principles of centrifugal force, if I swing this weight around over my head and let go, which direction will it fly?"

"A straight line tangent from the origin," Kyle answered easily.

"I guess you were paying attention," Mr. Meyer relented.

Kyle nodded, though he knew damn well it was dumb luck. He happened to have glanced over the passage before class, the only portion of last night's assigned reading that he'd actually looked at.

As the pride in his scholastic smackdown subsided, the realization that Luke's devotion was a figment of his imagination hit Kyle harder than the imaginary bully had. As much as the beginning of his mind's movie had sucked, the ending had made it totally worthwhile.

As he adjusted the boner that was very much rooted in reality, Kyle considered the implications of his football player fantasy. It was hot to have a man take a stand for him, care for him, and covet him. He wanted to be wanted like that. His new life in Tennessee was totally shitty, but the idea of having some testosterone-jacked hottie save him from it all was sexy as hell. He'd be a damsel in distress if it meant he would be wooed by a guy like Luke Larson.

Raking his fingers through his hair, Kyle struggled to focus, finding it impossible to stop swooning over the daydream. He didn't want to let it go, but he intermittently forced himself to focus on the chicken scratch Mr. Meyer was scrawling on the board. The only thing more depressing than the fact that his fantasy wasn't real was that he still had another thirteen minutes left in physics class. If he was going to be teased by a dream, he would have preferred it carried through until the end of the period. His premature rousing for nothing more than an endless succession of word problems was just cruel.

Kyle deserved a brain break, so he clocked out to thoughts of Luke's arms and how good it felt to have someone give a shit enough to take care of him, even if only in fantasy.

2

If waking up smack-dab in the middle of physics class hadn't been an exceedingly jarring reminder of his reality, passing Luke Larson in the hallway between sixth and seventh hour certainly was. Though it wasn't out of the ordinary for the jock to overlook him, Luke failing to spare a glance in Kyle's direction stung more than expected. His vivid dream had made Kyle believe, at least for a few stolen moments, that things were much better than they actually were. In his fantasies, he had Luke—a savior and a hotass who could get him out of Tennessee, and when he opened his eyes, he had nothing. Whether he was existing in a fantasy or in his new reality, Kyle couldn't ignore that even his dreams were riddled with pain, and the fact remained that there was nothing good in Iris Valley, Tennessee.

Months earlier—when the premature "midlife crisis" that had compelled his mother to leave his father had reached its climax—Hope Ross announced her intention to uproot her sons' lives in their well-to-do Dallas suburb in order to plant them in the dirt roads of a terrible Tennessee town. Upon receipt of the news, Kyle had been understandably livid, especially when considering the impetus for the impulsive change. His intelligent, hardworking mother had lost her fucking mind. Somewhere between business trips and being the family's breadwinner, Hope had decided she needed to "do something for herself." That "something" was chasing a decades-old love across the country and dragging her kids along for the ride. While the swiftness of his parents' divorce had been surprising, his mother's next steps were downright dizzying. In the span of a month, Kyle had gone from a popular, outgoing student to a withdrawn, bullied outcast.

Dealing with the divorce had been daunting, and the subsequent outcomes were too much for Kyle's seventeen-year-old heart to handle. To protect himself from further hurt, he'd folded in, arms wrapped around knees, hiding his vulnerabilities the best he could. He'd tuned out, toked up, and tried to get through the days as numb as possible. It was easier to cope with the bullshit when he was on a different plane of consciousness, so that's where he hung out whenever possible—somewhere between the past and present, but mostly above it all.

"Pass it," Kyle demanded as he sunk into the cognac leather couch beside his twin brother, Kris.

"Get your own," Kris huffed, dramatically turning his body away from Kyle's as he took a hit from the bowl in his hand.

"Really? You're not going to share?"

"I'm sick of sharing with your greedy ass. What do you do for me?"

Kyle gnawed on his lower lip, considering the question before he decided to double down on delusion. "Uh, everything."

"Everything?" Kris repeated, lifting his eyebrows high in amusement. "Since when?"

"Since always," Kyle decided, reaching over his brother's body in an attempt to grab the pipe Kris was holding just out of reach.

"Stop it."

"You stop it."

A sharp elbow to the ribs had Kyle yelping before glaring at his unapologetic twin.

Crossing his arms over his chest, Kyle sighed and gazed at the television, instantly annoyed by the crappy reality show Kris was watching. He didn't understand why his brother wasted time getting invested in the dysfunctional family featured in the series when he could simply reflect on the strangeness of their own situation and the arguments and anger it inspired. While Kyle didn't necessarily avoid drama, he couldn't help but find both the intensity and frequency of conflict in his household to be exhausting. There was no way around the tension, but that didn't mean he felt driven to exist within it.

"I had a bad day," Kyle said softly, strategically batting the lids of his doleful doe eyes. Though they shared features and expressions, Kyle found that pulling their signature pouty face could still trigger some semblance of sympathy from his brother.

Kris groaned and thrust the bowl into Kyle's waiting hands. "What's going on?"

"We still live here."

"So?"

"So that makes it a bad day," Kyle replied, bringing the pipe to his lips. A deep inhale filled his lungs with smoke before a sputtering cough sent it out of his mouth and into the moist basement air.

"I thought something specific happened."

"Our mother specifically moved us here to chase some dick who hardly gives her the time of day. Like..." Kyle shook his head, wondering if he'd be forever floored by his mother's odd behavior. "It would've been weird enough if she actually had a relationship with the guy, but the fact that she's just *trying* to have one...I can't wrap my head around it."

"She's 'doing something for me,'" Kris said, doing his best impression of his mother's defense. "She's 'spent years of my life devoting my energy to everyone else and now it's my time.'"

"Do you think she's bipolar or something? Maybe schizophrenic?" Kyle wondered, nudging Kris' knee and holding his hand out for the pipe.

"You can't diagnose people with mental illnesses because they make an odd decision. She's selfish."

"Narcissistic?"

Kris laughed. "That's still a mental illness."

"Moving your kids across the country in an attempt to mount some redneck isn't an 'odd decision,' it's a criminal offense."

"A criminal offense!" Kris cackled.

"It should be," Kyle stated plainly. The sound of his older brother, Matt, plodding down the basement stairs drew Kyle's attention, and he suddenly wished he was locked in his bedroom rather than sharing a communal space with his siblings. It wasn't that he didn't like his brothers, it was more that he couldn't stand them.

"Losers," Matt admonished, glancing from Kyle and Kris to the television and back again.

"Why are you down here if we're losers?" Kris retorted, kicking Matt's shin when he sat on the coffee table in front of them. "You're blocking the TV, dickbreath."

"You losers have weed," Matt replied, waving his hand for the bowl.

Reluctantly, Kyle handed the pipe to his brother, not in the mood to put up a fight.

Matt grinned and stood up only to plop himself down in the overstuffed chair next to the couch. "What are you chicks bitching about today?"

"This chick," Kris corrected, gesturing toward Kyle, "is complaining about Mom and the move."

"Same shit, different day, huh Kyle?" Matt remarked after blowing a plume of smoke from his nose. "You're just annoyed that you don't have your little army of admirers out here."

"You're bitter that you never had an army of admirers to begin with," Kyle shot back, standing up to grab the bowl from his brother's hand.

Though Kyle would never admit it, there was some truth to Matt's assertion. While he wouldn't exactly refer to his friends as an "army of admirers," he did miss having people around who gave a shit about what he had to say, thought everything he did was awesome, and laughed at his jokes. Honestly, he missed having friends at all. Transferring to a new school where he didn't know anyone in the middle of his junior year was a recipe for loneliness. So, he got baked as often as possible to cope with the feeling.

"I'm not even going to lie, I miss mine," Kris stated with a shrug.

"How can you miss a group of people who never existed?" Kyle laughed, dodging an attempted kick from his twin.

"Because you were the only one with friends, right?" Kris said defensively. "Is that what you're saying?"

Kyle took a quick hit and passed the weed to his brother. "You need this more than me."

"Don't you two get tired of being so annoying?" Matt wondered, leaning over to grab the remote from the arm of the couch. Switching the input, he retrieved the Xbox controller from between the cushions and started a single player game, unaffected by how bizarre his behavior was.

"Don't you get tired of being such a faggot?" Kris asked with a shit-eating grin, earning the middle finger from Matt.

While typically Kyle wouldn't flinch at the term they so casually tossed between them, thoughts of his dream earlier that day allowed the usage to provoke a pang of pain in his chest. He'd never let it hurt before. It was the most common insult at his previous school in Texas, and it certainly wasn't reserved for guys who were into other dudes. The last thing he wanted to do was grow sensitive over a word he'd never own.

"Says the biggest faggot I know," Matt scoffed.

Kyle rolled his eyes at their immaturity before leveling down with some of his own. "You're both faggots," he decided as he stood abruptly. He hadn't thought of what he'd do after he rose to his feet, so instead of provoking them further, he turned on his heels and headed up the stairs. He had better things to do than chill with their annoying asses.

Tossing himself down on his full-size bed, he stared up at the ceiling, attempting to come to terms with the fact that, unfortunately, he didn't have anything better to do. Fanning his fingers on his chest as he rolled his lips under his teeth, Kyle considered his options. The television in the basement had been bogarted and the one in the living room didn't have cable yet. He thought about getting online, but social media brought him down. The last thing he wanted to do was look at pictures of all his friends having a good time in Texas while he was rotting in Bumfuck, Egypt. Though he regretted impulsively leaving the couch and weed, he refused to go back downstairs to hang out with those dumbasses.

The needy straining in his groin urged him to kill time and benefit from some natural stress relief. Tucking his hand below the waistband of his boxer briefs, Kyle began to fondle his cock, grinning when it responded immediately to the touch. In a world full of constant disappointments, his dick never let him down. Shimmying himself free, he closed his eyes and implored his mind to recreate the fantasy it had so brilliantly produced about Luke Larson. As he increased the speed of his wrist, he thought of being tossed over the shoulder of the titan, cared for like he was a child. He wanted to be cosseted like that. Vividly imagined kisses sent Kyle over the edge and he frantically reached for the tissues he had on his nightstand.

Throwing the wad of paper onto the ground beside his bed, Kyle curled up into the fetal position and closed his eyes. A nap sounded nice.

3

While Kyle always knew he was intelligent, he never felt like a genius until he began attending Iris Valley High School. Putting forth a minimal amount of effort, he easily earned exemplar marks—an impossibility at West River High. His former school was top-notch, with tuned-in teachers and a strong PTA full of families with fat wallets and high expectations. Though he didn't realize it at the time, Kyle had been lucky to attend a school of that caliber. It was easy to see what he lost after it was gone, especially since he had the opposite at his new school. Nobody gave a damn about anything at IVHS—not the administration, teachers, and least of all the students. Kyle wondered what his life would have been like if he'd grown up in rural Tennessee rather than an affluent suburb of Texas and attended a school that didn't give him the attention he so desperately sought in his younger years.

When Kyle recalled his middle school experience, he wanted to shake himself for being so entitled. His parents had been so preoccupied with their busy and lucrative careers that Kyle, Kris, and Matt were mostly raised by nannies who understandably had to split their time between the three of them. Feeling shafted by the lack of explicit attention, Kyle acted out in school, doing dumb stuff like flipping chairs on their backs and calling out in class. Predictably, the immature antics garnered the reactions he was looking for, and any regard was better than the disregard he'd gotten at home. He spent a significant amount of time in the Principal's office, and despite his propensity to perturb teachers, Principal Morris seemed to enjoy their time together, shaking his head with a smirk on his lips when Kyle would show up yet again.

West River Unified School District worked as hard as many of the community's parents to raise the children to be upstanding members of society. Their curriculum was constructed around the six pillars of character: trustworthiness, respect, responsibility, fairness, caring, and citizenship. Regardless of how naughty Kyle was in class, the values he learned at West River were engrained in him far beyond the school's hallways.

Though at his core, Kyle still craved attention the way he had in Texas, he found it so disconcerting to have strangers' eyes on him in Tennessee that he did everything he could to fade into the background, become nothing more than a nameless face. It was a hard truth to acknowledge, that he was the outcast he would have made fun of back at West River, a fact that put his past behavior in perspective. Though it had only been two months since the move, Kyle was no longer the person he'd been before. He'd never realized how intricately West River was woven into the fibers of his personality until he was away from his hometown and barely able to recognize himself. He didn't like being withdrawn or worried about being seen. It was strange to be homesick, not only for a place but for the person he was before.

A knock on his bedroom door halted Kyle's negative train of thought, an interruption he would've been grateful for if it wasn't obvious what the expectation would be.

"Why knock when you're just going to walk in?" Kyle asked as Hope entered the room.

"Why ask when you know it doesn't make a difference, she retorted. "Why aren't you dressed?

"Uh," Kyle sighed, staring at his closet as if he could somehow telepathically get himself ready for school just by focusing on that area of his room. It was unlike him to feel unmotivated to put an effort into his appearance. It had always been a source of pride, how well he took care of himself, how organized he was, and how clean-cut. He relished in the appreciation he received from his former classmates who noticed how well he kept it together. Not wanting to be seen put a kink in his typical routine, and he had a harder time than usual getting out of bed in the morning.

"Hurry up," she urged. "You need to eat breakfast. You're too skinny."

"Maybe if we had decent food to eat, I would. Plus, you birthed me, so it's your fault," he retorted. He bit his tongue in an attempt to stop himself from going for her guts, his first impulse.

"Bullshit," she disagreed. "Boys shouldn't be so small. You need to put some meat on that bony body. Girls won't give you a second look if you're smaller than them."

If it wasn't for his physics class fantasy the day before, his mother's comments would have easily rolled off Kyle's back, but his subconscious craving for care had him feeling more vulnerable than was typical.

Hope's ignorant disregard of the chance that Kyle may be disinterested in girls' impressions of him was bothersome. Was it so wrong for a guy to want to be protected and coveted by another guy? A connection that was so natural in his dreams wasn't even acknowledged as a *possibility* in heteros' hypotheticals. It was as though it was so outside the norm that the possibility was offensive. Kyle had spent the majority of his adolescence subscribing to the same stalled train of thought, thinking that he had to be a certain way, draw a specific type of attention from the "fairer" sex. He was fair too, and he wanted to be treated that way.

The one time he'd been with a guy hadn't been particularly soft or romantic, and though it had felt good to have a mouth on his dick, the whole vibe was kind of weird. It was more functional than sexy, like they were both working for the outcome rather than enjoying the ride. It had convinced him that he wasn't as into guys as his body seemed to think it was. That was what he wanted to believe anyway. There was no doubt his life would be easier if he was a regular teenage dude who drooled over tits rather than toned pectorals. Still, no matter how much he tried pretend he wasn't who he was, hotties like Luke Larson assured him that his attempts to be anything but gay were futile.

"What if I don't like girls?" he muttered mostly to himself. The most brazen layer of his brain hoped his mother would hear him and that the admission would piss her off. But his rational mind knew that it wasn't the time, and it probably never would be.

"What?" Hope asked, crinkling her nose as if she was trying to discern what he'd said.

"Nothing," Kyle replied, loud and clear. "You can leave, I'm changing."

Kyle waited until his mother closed the door behind her before climbing out of bed. He didn't bother to check his phone like he would have if he was still in West River. Hardly anyone texted him anymore. Out of sight, out of mind. After putting on a black t-shirt and grey hoodie and yanking a pair of fitted jeans over his slim legs, Kyle glanced in the full-length mirror behind his door. He looked better than most in that horse-piss town ever would. Good enough. He washed his face, brushed his teeth, and took a piss before heading down the stairs to the kitchen, where he was the last to arrive at the breakfast table and eventually the first to excuse himself.

"Get in the car," Hope directed as Kyle slung his backpack over his shoulder.

Kyle had spent the majority of his childhood wishing his mother were around more than she was and a good chunk of the time in Tennessee preferring she wasn't. He'd spent years in nannies' arms while glorifying his mother's, only to realize with time that they were as weak as he was strong. It was terrible to consider that perhaps they were always that way, even when she'd made him feel like her embrace was the safest place in the world. Maybe at some point she had been, and everything had changed. Maybe that's why he felt so jilted, because he'd had her attention before he didn't. He knew what he was missing.

Kyle nodded and leaned against the cabinets as he waited for everyone to finish eating. He considered pulling out his History book to review that week's chapters prior to the test he had later that morning, but ultimately decided against it. The class would no doubt pester Ms. Johnston into making the exam open-book, and the teacher would relent, just as she always did. While he didn't see the point of taking a test if he didn't actually need to know the information, he wasn't about to complain. He did, however, consider the long-term ramifications for his classmates who didn't have the strong academic foundation that West River gave him. Of course, they didn't seem concerned, but that was what a shitty education did to people; it made them ignorant of how much they didn't know.

"Why are you hovering?" Kris chided, glaring over his shoulder at Kyle. "You're making me nervous."

"It's not hovering if I'm, like, five feet away, dumbass," Kyle scoffed, crinkling his nose at the stupid comment. "You belong here."

"What's that supposed to mean?" Kris demanded.

"Iris Valley. You belong here. You fit in with our asinine classmates," Kyle clarified.

Kris rolled his eyes. "You're such a little bitch. We get to do whatever we want here, and all you do is complain about it. You constantly react to mundane comments with, like, this global narrative about the detriments of society."

"Oh come on!" Matt laughed, nearly choking on his bacon. "You strung together a bunch of big words trying to make yourself look smart."

"They aren't big words," Kris huffed. "If you think they are, maybe *you* belong here."

"Hypocrite," Kyle noted. "You just did the same thing you gave me crap about."

"No, I didn't," Kris disagreed, placing his plate in the sink.

"You did," Matt asserted.

They walked out to the porch with Hope following close behind.

"Is this the new insult? That someone belongs here?" Hope questioned, clearly unimpressed with the development. "Don't talk badly about these people. They're nice people. You're going to know them all for the rest of your life. Believe me. You won't be in touch with the people you grew up with, but these people, you'll be in touch with them."

Kyle laughed despite himself, taking a drag of the Newport Light Kris handed him.

"Besides, it's beautiful here. I leave the house every morning and I'm in awe of how lush the landscape is," she continued.

"Yeah mom, it's beautiful, but there's nothing to fucking do..." Kyle grumbled, shaking his head at how willfully obtuse she was, "but yeah the trees are nice." He tuned out her inevitably annoying response, resting his forehead in the palm of his hand for a moment before abruptly announcing: "I'm walking."

"Why would you walk two miles when you have a ride?" Hope cried with an exasperated sigh.

"It's nice out," Kyle said. And it was. The crisp October air fanned through his hair as he took the porch steps by twos.

"You owe me a cigarette, asshole," Kris called after him.

As Kyle ambled down the winding country road toward school, he made a concerted effort not to admire the wide umbrella of stone-fruit-toned leaves adorning the long limbs of maple trees above him. There was no beauty in betrayal.

4

Several hours and one open-book test later, Kyle sat at a table, picking aimlessly at a plate of crinkle-cut french fries. It was difficult to work up an appetite when his stomach began churning every time he walked into the cafeteria. He dreaded that moment when he would inevitably take a seat at a table in the corner of the room, hoping miraculously someone would show him some mercy and sit on the empty chair across from him. The only person who ever did was Kris, and that was a sporadic occurrence due to his brother's near constant assignment to lunch detention.

The ostracization had driven him to consider the cliché teenage nightmare of choking down his meal in a bathroom stall. Though he would be relieved to be *purposely* alone, the idea of attempting to eat on a toilet was more unappealing than trying to ingest the shitty french fries in the first place. It was ironic that they tasted how he felt about Tennessee, cold and salty. He knew he needed to get over it. It was exhausting to be constantly angry, yet he hadn't found a way to effectively abate the dark emotions. From the smile on Kris' face as he crossed the room toward Kyle, it was obvious he'd found a way to move past the awfulness, at least temporarily.

"Hey, fag! How was the walk?" Kris asked, immediately grabbing a fry off Kyle's plate.

Having lost his appetite thanks to the soggy sticks, Kyle cringed as Kris continuously shoveled them in.

"Fine," Kyle replied, taking a swig of his Coke and sloshing it around the inside of his cheeks in an attempt to rid his mouth of the fries' aftertaste.

"That was totally one of those immature things you do when you're pissed. You think you'll get some sort of reaction but really, nobody gives a fuck, and you're just punishing yourself."

"Hmm," Kyle hummed, focusing on the contents of the tray that was now fully in front of his brother. "Speaking of punishing yourself..."

"It's called eating," Kris snarked. "You put something in your mouth, mash it up with these sharp things sticking out of your gums called teeth, then ingest the food to give your body nutrients and energy."

As Kyle glared at his twin, unimpressed, Kris continued:

"You should try it sometime. Mom's not right about a lot of things but she's not a total idiot. You do look too thin."

Aggravated, Kyle punched out a heavy sigh. "We're literally identical. How about you worry about your own scrawny body and I'll take care of mine?"

"I've got three pounds on you," Kris stated.

"So that makes you an expert on health and well-being? Remember who's older and wiser."

"Yes, because our parents have really proven time and time again that with age comes wisdom," Kris laughed. "Your extra nine minutes on Earth instantly made you a sage."

"Pretty much," Kyle confirmed, grinning at his brother. The smile dropped when he considered Kris' words. The last thing he wanted to do was lose weight, knowing how difficult it would be to gain it back. As if he didn't have enough to worry about, his inability to put on pounds and achieve the athletic physique he desired was an immutable irritation.

"Eat or don't eat. I don't care. We have more important things to talk about."

"Oh yeah?" Kyle wondered.

"Mm-hmm. I figured out a way to get out of Tennessee."

Raising an interested eyebrow, Kyle gestured for Kris to continue.

"Weed."

"What?"

"We need to start selling weed," his brother stated flatly, as if becoming drug dealers would alleviate all their issues and be the answer to every future problem they may encounter.

"We need to start selling weed," Kyle repeated slowly, trying to read Kris' expression and discern whether he was kidding, or if he had, in fact, lost his mind. "Are you serious?"

"Absolutely."

"How does that even help?" he scoffed.

"We'll be able to sock away some money, and as soon as we turn eighteen, we can move back to Texas." Kris snapped his fingers for emphasis and smiled like he hadn't just proposed they join the drug game in order to get out of Tennessee *eventually*.

"That's in two years," Kyle noted, chiding himself for being disappointed that the "important conversation" was bunk.

"I know how to count," Kris retorted. "I'm serious, Kyle. Think about it. We save up a little bit of cash, and then we go back to Dallas like straight ballers. We can get a nice place in Austin, pull a bunch of college pussy..."

Straight? Pussy? It still sounded more appealing to Kyle than Iris Valley. "I thought you were going to tell me something way more immediate than this."

"Like what?"

Kyle shrugged. "I don't know, giving Mom a basement lobotomy or something."

"Yeah," Kris chuckled, "because that's a lot more realistic than saving up to get a place in the future."

"Saving up for a place by selling drugs," Kyle whispered, peeking over his shoulder as if anyone was actually close enough to hear what he'd said.

"Since when are you such a Boy Scout?" Kris questioned.

"We *were* Boy Scouts," Kyle smirked. The mere mention of their scouting days reminded him of Richard Markman, and how he really should give his old friend a call.

"We got kicked out of the troop for lighting that trashcan in the rec room on fire," Kris noted. "Even as Boy Scouts we were smoking people out." He reached across the table to playfully pinch Kyle's cheek.

Kyle held his fist out so Kris could bump it. "Worth it."

"So what do you think?" Kris continued. "Do you want to get rich?"

Though selling weed was morally ambiguous, thanks to the illegality and a social stigma surrounding those who peddled pot, Kyle reasoned that it wasn't legal to smoke it either and he did a fair bit of that. Not only was he already a consumer, he was an avid one. And it wasn't like he'd be selling crack or meth. "I don't know. I don't want to end up in prison."

"You're not black," Kris reminded. "White kids get away with shit black kids never would."

"Alright."

"You're in?" Kris asked surprised. "I never thought you'd agree to it."

Kyle narrowed his eyes. "Are you chickening out as soon as I tell you I'm into it?"

"Well, no..." Kris began, scratching the back of his head, "but I literally just thought of this while I was taking a shit during fifth period. I don't have any idea how we'll even get started."

"It can't be that difficult."

"Where do we get the weed?"

"We can get it from Johnny," Kyle suggested. "We buy it low and then charge people more than he does."

"Yeah, then when he realizes what we're doing he'll kill us," Kris said, pursing his lips. "That's how shit happens on the streets."

"Johnny's the laziest stoner in existence. He won't do anything."

"Fine, maybe not, but why would people pay us more for the same product he's selling for less?"

"You used to be entrepreneurial," Kyle admonished, recalling the many "businesses" he and Kris ran as kids. Whether it was selling candy to classmates at school or begging their nanny to set up a lemonade stand in the front yard of their West River home, they were hustlers.

"Used to be? Who came up with the idea?" Kris exclaimed, tossing one of the final french fries at Kyle's face.

"You can have tons of ideas, but if you don't know how to follow through with them you're a philosopher, not a businessman," Kyle stated, narrowing his eyes at his brother. "So I'm the boss, and you're the..."

"Brains?" Kris offered.

"Braun," Kyle corrected. "Since you have three pounds on me now."

Kris tsked but didn't argue. Instead, he reached his hand across the table. "So we're in business then?"

"We're in business," Kyle confirmed as he shook his twin's hand.

"All we need now is the product and a plan."

"I'll handle it all," Kyle promised. "And while I'm doing that, you can try to get friendly with some stoners so we'll have customers when we're ready to go."

"I'm already friendly with a bunch of dudes."

"Get friendly with more, faggot," Kyle suggested, nodding toward a group of grungy looking kids sitting at a table diagonal from theirs.

Kris grinned. "I'm on it."

As Kyle watched his brother assimilate into the group, he reminisced about how nice it had been not to be an outcast. It was a feeling that had become so foreign to him that he typically didn't dare allow himself to think of his friends for more than a few seconds, finding it too painful to miss what he no longer had. Somehow, the excitement of his new business venture helped Kyle handle the nostalgia better than he usually did and compelled him to pull his phone out and toggle to Richard's name.

Kyle (12:43pm): Hey, how are you?

Richard (12:45pm): Holy moly! You're alive! It's been too long. I'm doing well. How are you?

Kyle (12:46pm): Fine.

Richard (12:46pm): You seemed gloomy about everything the last time we talked. Are things better now?

Kyle (12:47pm): It's not home, but it's cool. Not a big deal.

Richard (12:47pm): You play everything off. You're allowed to have emotions about it.

Kyle (12:47pm): I have a lot of emotions about it.

Richard (12:48pm): Well, you're allowed to share them then.

Kyle (12:48pm): What if once I start I can't stop? How do I handle it then?

Richard (12:49pm): One day at a time. It may take a while, but things will get better, and maybe one day it will feel like home.

Kyle (12:50pm): I just wanted to say hi.

Richard (12:50pm): Hi.

Kyle (12:51pm): Hi Richard.

Richard (12:51pm): Now that that's over with, tell me what you've been up to for the past month.

Kyle (12:52pm): I'd rather tell you over the phone. How about I give you a call later?

Richard (12:52pm): Later as in this afternoon, or another four weeks?

Kyle (12:53pm): Oh c'mon...

Kyle didn't have the heart to admit it would be a while. He couldn't afford to be raw and he already felt his guard dropping. Sliding his phone back into his back pocket, Kyle cleared his tray, gave Kris one last glance and climbed the stairs to hide in the bathroom for the rest of the period.

5

It was rare that Hope was home at night. The majority of her evenings were spent at Jimmy's place, a pattern that only aggravated Kyle when he was feeling particularly angry about the move to Tennessee. It was bizarre that his mother spent most of her days handpicking pounds of beans before standing by the stovetop preparing them. She touted that they were the best beans anyone ever ate, but Kyle thought they tasted the same as other variations of the fart-y food. While her new appreciation for beans was strange, her foray into making apple pie moonshine was something Kyle could get behind, if only because the mason jars of cloudy amber liquid adorned with cinnamon sticks got him wasted off his ass.

While Kyle maintained a predominantly pissed off affect, there were odd moments of reprieve where he appreciated the freedoms his mother's near-constant absence allowed him. However, Hope's daily commitment to show up in their kitchen before school perturbed Kyle beyond any reasonable level of decompression. Try as he might, once he caught sight of his mother sitting at the table as if she belonged there, he instantly became irritated by the ruse of responsible parenting. He would have preferred if she didn't put forth the pointless effort and stayed at Jimmy's for good.

"You know what I was thinking?" she began, busting into Kyle's room sometime after nine at night. Her presence in the house, and subsequent appearance in his room nearly knocked him off his bed.

"What the fuck, mom?" he growled, tugging his earbuds out and narrowing his eyes at Hope. "Why are you here?"

"I live here," she said so matter-of-factly that Kyle was sure she actually believed it to be true. Any other time he would have come back with a quip, but he was too curious about what she was doing standing in the middle of his room to risk distracting from the explanation. "I think I'm going to redo those bedrooms in the basement so you and your brothers can have your own space down there. We'll do it up really nicely. It will be like your own apartment."

"We have the whole house," Kyle stated with a wry laugh. "Are you serious?"

"There's no winning with you," Hope sighed, throwing her hands up in the air, exasperated.

"You're so dramatic."

"I'm dramatic?" she scoffed. "I'm not the one who's been dragging my bottom lip around on the ground, becoming a professional pouter."

Crinkling his nose, Kyle glared at his mother. "I have plenty of reasons to be pissed."

"Well, I'm trying to give you one less reason," Hope explained. "I'll let you pick your own paint color."

"How does this benefit you?" he asked skeptically.

"I spent *years* of my life putting everyone else first. Now, I make *one* decision to follow my heart and put my feelings first, and you act like I've never prioritized you or done anything simply to please you and your brothers."

"And this is it?" Kyle yawned, wishing he had the capacity to drop it, to ignore his mother's newfound martyrdom. "I don't feel like doing this right now, Mom."

"But it's all you do," she contended, with her hands on her hips and emotions brimming on the waterline of her eyes. "You're relentless."

"I'm realistic," he corrected. "Every decision you've made will forever change the person I am. I can't imagine having that kind of power and not making the best decisions I could."

"And you don't think your decisions impact me?" Hope retorted. "You don't think your disenchantment changes me?"

Pressing his thumb and forefinger against the depression of his eye sockets, Kyle shook his head. "Why are you here?"

"In Tennessee or your room?" she attempted to clarify.

"In the house in general."

Hope huffed, punching out a peeved sigh. "You'll understand it one day when you fall in love. You'll meet a girl who makes you want to move mountains and then you'll get it."

"What if I don't?" Kyle challenged, thoughts of his lack of thought about girls pervading his mind. Despite how often his mother brought up women, Kyle never imagined himself with one. Instead he was stuck thinking about wide-chested jocks like Luke Larson. He should have been coveting a humdrum hetero relationship, maybe then Tennessee wouldn't be such a mindfuck. Maybe he would've knocked up some local within months of graduation and spent his life working at a gas station so he could keep the trailer roof over her head. Maybe he would've barely had the bills paid before she got pregnant again, and he'd have grown to hate her as much as he hated himself. Maybe he would fit in one day if he stopped being who he was and started being who his mother wanted him to be.

"What if you don't what?"

"What if I don't meet a girl I want to move mountains for or whatever?"

Hope clicked her tongue. "People can be whoever they want to be once they're successful, before that..." she shook her head. "Nobody should make rash decisions before they're indispensable. You have to know you're solid before you start rocking the boat."

"I have no idea what you're talking about," Kyle stated, but the ache in his chest reminded him it was a lie. There were things they both needed to come to terms with, uncomfortable truths made more challenging by the forced isolation. Something had to give, and Kyle was pretty sure it would be him.

"Are you going to tell me what you think about the basement renovation or what?" she demanded, visibly pressed by the conversation.

"I think if it would make you feel like less of a failure, you should do it."

"A failure," Hope scoffed, her lips pursed tight. "Failures don't build careers like I did, Kyle."

"But they lose their jobs," he said, immediately regretting the statement when he saw the hurt on his mother's face.

In typical Hope fashion, she swallowed her words and attempted to decimate him with her dark brown eyes. "Think about what color you want for the walls," she directed, before turning to exit the room. "You're just like your father."

Kyle was positive his mother meant the statement as an insult, but in his mind, being told he was like his father was anything but slander. Unlike Hope, Ken was even-tempered and consistent. While his mother was in the throes of a midlife crisis, his father was steady, living in a lake town two hours east of West River. There was no doubt in Kyle's mind that his dad was enjoying the quiet. Maybe that's why they spoke so infrequently. While it was easy for Kyle to blame Hope for her indiscretions, he found it nearly impossible to do the same for Ken.

Whether he saw his father as the victim of his mother's poor decisions was neither here nor there. Kyle had always striven to gain his father's favor, to make the discerning man proud. The forced physical distance between them strapped Kyle with a handicap that made the goal unreachable. What would he tell him on the phone? That he was the smartest kid in a school full of inbreds? That he was considering getting into dealing to get out of Tennessee? Iris Valley didn't leave Kyle with much to boast about. He wondered what Hope got out of it. Before moving to Appalachia, Hope had lived the luxurious life, traveling and wearing the best brands. It was difficult for Kyle to correlate the woman standing in the middle of his room with the one who had owned boardrooms. What had happened to her? How had a lowlife like Jimmy had enough pull to take her away from her swanky suburb? Kyle knew that being laid off from her corporate career had been a blow to her ego, but he never imagined such an accomplished woman would sink so low. Perhaps there was more to it than he understood, but the three weeks he'd spent in Jimmy's home when they first moved to Tennessee had been enough for Kyle to have his own opinions on the situation.

Though Hope had assured the boys that the living arrangements were temporary, Kyle hadn't been convinced. It seemed suspect to move across the country to be with a guy and then settle into that same man's house. He hadn't believed there was any way Hope would actually leave, and while it was debatable that she ever really did, she had been truthful about the fact that she'd purchased a house and was having it renovated during the three weeks they lived with Jimmy.

"Like I said, you can choose the paint colors," Hope said curtly, regarding Kyle like a sales agent with no incentive.

"Alright."

"You're the hardest on me," Hope stated. "Do you know that? Your brothers have shown they have the capacity to forgive, forget, or simply forge forward, and you've displayed nothing of the sort."

Kyle clicked his tongue. "I'm not fake."

"But you're bitter," she pointed out, "and all bitterness does is rot you from the inside."

"I'll be okay," he promised, securing the buds in his ears. He could feel his heart pounding against his chest cavity and the bothersome choppiness of his breath. He hated that comments from his mother could still invoke the physical reaction that they did, that he was somehow under her power though he felt so far removed.

He heard her muffled directive to think about what color he wanted beyond the beat of the music that was flooding his ears. And though he considered telling her right off the bat that he wanted black, navy or some other color that would be a nightmare to paint over, Kyle decided against it. There was so much more time for torture. All he wanted to do after his long day was sleep.

Hope got the message, mumbling her inaudible aggravation before exiting the room. While Kyle had never considered his third-floor bedroom easily breached, the mere presence of his mother past the nine o'clock hour was compelling enough to make him seriously consider her basement proposal.

"So what are you going to do with our rooms?" Kyle asked. "If you're moving us all to the basement."

"Well, I was thinking of using Matt's room to expand the master and then combining yours and Kris' to make a nice guest room."

"Who the fuck is coming to Hell to stay with us?"

Hope rolled her eyes. "Hell?"

He shrugged.

"Gaining more independence is hardly a bad thing, son. This will be a good thing, right?"

Fighting his gut reaction to accuse his mother of attempting to displace him and his brothers, Kyle kept his lips pursed tight. He had to weigh the positives, and there was no denying there were a lot of them, especially after Kris' proposal earlier that day. The basement had private entry. The idea of all of them being down there to look over their "business" was appealing.

"Right," Kyle decided, and his first idea was to paint his room green—the color of the weed he was going to sell.

Though he wasn't completely enamored of the idea of being banished to the basement by his mother, it was cool to imagine how awesome the space could be if he started making a lot of dough. Not only could they upgrade their gaming system, they could get a badass projector and surround sound to raise the experience to the next level. Instead of the Goodwill couch they had, they'd spring for a black leather sectional with electric recliners and built-in cup holders to hold the bottles of imported beer they'd have lining the backlit shelves above the brand new wet bar. Tennessee would still suck, but the basement would be their refuge.

"So it's settled," Hope stated, her affect as low as he'd seen it in months.

Kyle liked it that way.

6

Despite Kris' concerns, it wasn't difficult for Kyle to come up with a plan that differentiated them from other dealers. He figured that the best way to obtain and then retain customers was to give them an experience that the other guys didn't have the foresight or business savvy to offer. Instead of passing dime bags to dudes in the school parking lot, Kyle invited them to the basement, where he and Kris smoked them up then sent them away with an overpriced gram.

As expected, the little bit of hospitality went a long way. Their basement, which had formerly been frequented by only the three brothers, was now a hub for Iris Valley's most popular students. Kris enjoyed the upgrade, while Kyle appreciated the money that came from purchases much more than he liked the people making them. Still, there was something to be said for the semblance of respect they garnered for selling. It was odd to be as isolated as they had been, and having groups of kids around them was a sliver of normalcy, even though dealing wasn't.

"We sold another bag," Kris whispered, the surprise evident in his voice. Kyle wondered how long it would take for Kris to realize that their model was legit and that they should assume sales would flood in rather than being awestruck by them.

"Of course we did," Kyle scoffed, shoving the cash Kris handed him into the back pocket of his jeans. "Look at them," he gestured to three classmates sitting pleasantly baked on the couch, "those are some happy customers."

"What if Johnny catches on to what we're doing and refuses to sell us weed?" Kris pressed.

"That's not going to happen," Kyle answered easily, "and even if he does, there are tons of other Johnnys. We'll find shit to buy, and it'll probably be better quality."

"Since when are you such an optimist," Kris teased.

"Since my pocket's packed with cash," Kyle grinned, patting the stack in his jeans for effect. "There's something to it."

"You're just happy to have a couple more ounces when you weigh yourself."

"I never weigh myself, Mom," Kyle bristled. "Is this the new obsession? My weight? There have to be other things you pricks can think about."

"Did you call Mom a prick?" Matt asked with a Twizzler hanging out of his mouth and a beer in his hand.

"I've called her a lot of things, but prick isn't one of them," Kyle said, averting his eyes from the nearly catatonic, busty blonde drinking him in from the couch.

"She'd break you in half," Kris stated, waving at the girl, who immediately glanced away. "We're identical," he informed her loudly, clicking his tongue. "Is she serious?"

Kyle shrugged. "I have a way with women, I guess."

"Most faggots do," Kris nodded. "That's typical, right?"

"You're always looking for an excuse for your lack of game," Matt interjected. "Is this your new one?"

"You would stick up for him," Kris laughed, shaking his head. "When he's so undeserving..."

Kyle rolled his eyes. "Want me to tell you what you deserve?"

"The world?" Kris smirked. "I agree."

"Cocky little monkey," Matt chided. "You know, sometimes I lay awake at night trying to figure out who's cockier, you or Kyle?"

"And what'd you come up with?" Kris wondered.

"In Texas it's Kyle, no doubt, but here it's definitely you," Matt told Kris. "He lost his swagger."

"I lost hope, not my swagger," Kyle corrected.

"But we still have 'Hope,'" Matt smirked, happy to get a chance to play with his favorite pun, "at least in the mornings."

Kyle rolled his eyes. "Are you ever going to stop being corny?"

"Are you ever going to get over yourself?" his older brother retorted.

Though Kyle knew the question was nothing more than the typical jab, he couldn't help but reflect on the sentiment. His self-esteem had always been healthy, but his short time in Tennessee had depleted it greatly. He'd never dealt with feeling like an outcast before, and the isolation had made him reflect on his flaws more than he had in the past. It's second nature to wonder what's wrong with you when everyone looks at you like something is. Kyle hated that somehow he'd developed a complex about shit he'd hardly thought about before. He'd never thought of himself as diminutive, but that seemed to be everyone's impression of him, and his mother's buy-in was disenchanting. He didn't want to perseverate on inane thoughts of inadequacy because he was built with a smaller frame than most boys. It had never felt as impactful as it did in Tennessee, like his slight body was somehow an analogy for the power of his presence. Things would change. He knew that. Any man was tall when he stood on his money, when bills broadened his back.

"Are you?" Kris interjected, glaring at Matt. Kris and Kyle didn't often get along, but when they did, it was usually because they were messing with Matt.

Matt rolled his eyes before taking the basement stairs by twos. The sound of clanking pots confirmed what Kyle had suspected, it was almost macaroni and cheese time. As uninspired as Matt's dinner offerings were, Kyle was glad he made the effort to fix something. The weed business had been surprisingly time-consuming, and though they were only a week into the new venture, it was obvious they needed to divide and conquer when it came to the household tasks.

Hope had pushed forward with her basement renovation timeline, which was problematic considering that Kyle was trying to entertain his customers in the space. The last thing he wanted to do was have a lull in business right when they were establishing themselves. Though Kyle had thought about dealing on the main floor given how infrequently Hope was home in the afternoons, his brothers had convinced him that all it would take was one unannounced homecoming to end what they were working hard to build. Kyle figured they were better off allowing interruptions for a few weeks than getting risky right out of the gate.

The fact that he even had to consider his mother's feelings infuriated him, especially given how infrequently she seemed to worry about his. The only consistent concern she displayed was a displeasure in his "famished" frame. She'd had the audacity to ask him if he was eating, a question he promptly scoffed at. Secretly he tucked his balls in to stop himself from busting hers, dying to remind her of how seldom she cooked dinner. For someone who was so worried about his slight stature, Hope was awfully out of touch with his consumption. Though she still made it home in the mornings to see them off to school, she wasn't there for long enough to scramble eggs or flip bacon. Kyle was over the charade and entirely sick of her. He wondered if his brothers felt the same frustration he did just from looking at her face. If they did, they hid it well. He knew they were angry about the move to Tennessee, but Kris and Matt had managed to adjust to the area quicker than Kyle ever could have.

"You know," Kris began, "It wouldn't be a big deal for us to move the operation upstairs temporarily while they work down here."

"You've given me shit for half the day when I suggested the exact same thing," Kyle remarked, shaking his head.

"You're annoying as shit, you know that?" Kris huffed.

"Is shit annoying?" Kyle smirked. "Like, I could rattle off a list of annoying things, and I don't think I'd put 'shit' on it."

Kris rolled his eyes and crossed his arms over his chest. "So, you don't want to go on hiatus anymore?"

Playfully tapping the wad of cash in his twin's back pocket, Kyle clicked his tongue. "Not a chance. Worse comes to worse, she catches us and then what?" He shrugged. "She probably wouldn't focus on us for long enough to realize what we're doing."

"Is this some twisted mommy fantasy that you're getting me wrapped up in? Some attention-seeking behavior?"

"The last thing I want is her attention," Kyle scoffed, well aware that he was lying. It was an odd paradox to crave something he dreaded. "That's the last thing I want," he repeated impotently.

"Whatever you have to tell yourself to get through the night, fag," Kris shrugged. "It would make you more of a man to admit you miss your mommy." The way he sang the title made Kyle want to punch him in his smug face.

"You act like a four year old."

"A four year old with a stack of cash in his pocket," Kris corrected.

"I can't think of anything more dangerous."

"Sure you could. How about a sixteen year old?" Raising his eyebrows, Kris gave Kyle their most mischievous look.

"That's even worse," Kyle relented with a grin. "What are you thinking?"

"I'm thinking we should reinvest, pour it back into the business."

"And do what? Buy higher quality weed or something?" Kyle asked skeptically. As far as he was concerned, buying twenty-eight grams of mids for a hundred and twenty dollars and then selling the grams for ten bucks was good enough. They were making a hundred and sixty dollars on every bag they bought from Johnny. There was no denying that the quality wasn't as good as the stuff they got in Dallas, but everything was shittier in Tennessee. It stopped being surprising months ago.

"I was thinking we could segue into something harder," Kris replied, gesturing to the naked couple on the couch. "It wouldn't be hard to push some perk-me-ups on a bunch of faded people."

"We have to get better at what we're doing now before we put more on our plate," Kyle chided. "You literally know nothing."

"This was all my idea," Kris reminded. "You would've never even considered it without me."

"Yeah, well thanks for your corruption."

"Oh yeah, because you were such a pure person before."

"Like an angel," Kyle smirked.

"Every administrator at West River High School disagrees."

"They just wanted to hang out with me because I'm so charming," Kyle said, giving his twin a cheeky grin.

Kris sighed nostalgically. "The good old days, huh?"

Kyle nodded. The good old days.

7

There were times when everything felt like it was moving too quickly, like the days and years were passing in the blink of an eye. While Kyle rarely pined for the past beyond merely missing Texas, certain memories that stood out to him and made him long for moments that hadn't seemed as impactful to him at the time but became more meaningful with the months.

Though Kris aggravated him, Kyle couldn't help but acknowledge how frequently the times worth remembering featured his twin. It was strange how entwined they were even when Kyle felt thousands of miles from Kris. Often it was as if his brother had made the move to Tennessee, and Kyle had stayed back in West River, hoping for some actual change as he enjoyed the days in the only place he'd ever considered home.

So much of Kyle's being was defined by his brother. There was something powerful about sharing everything with Kris from conception. It went deeper than their eyes, noses, or mouths; it was their blood and soul, so much to bind them even when they stood ideologically apart. With the years, space had naturally wedged its way between them even when they were reluctant to allow it. Sometimes Kyle wondered what their relationship would be like in the future. If years could slowly pull them apart, what would decades do? Would they live far from one another? Have different friends? Take completely different paths?

While Kyle rarely perseverated on what *could* be, in his most anxious moments, he worried that memories shared between him and Kris would fade away, eraser curls blown to the floor. There was so much he didn't want to forget, things that made him feel warm, even when he wanted to act coldly toward his brother. Every time Kris gave Hope a pass, Kyle felt the chill of betrayal. Though he'd never admit it, Kris' acceptance forced Kyle to consider that perhaps he was somehow overreacting, that maybe his mother wasn't as awful as his actions made her seem. The mere chance that Kyle was overreacting had him rationalizing his disapproval, thus liking his mother less than he had before. It was a destructive cycle that always left him more disillusioned than he was before. Not for nothing, he grasped his anger tight, happy to hold on as long as it took, knowing damn well that no matter how long he did, he wouldn't change his mother's mind. She was Tennessee or die, and die was exactly what Kyle would prefer to do if he had to stay in the landlocked state any longer. The only thing he could do to mitigate the malaise was daydream of simpler days.

It was easy for Kyle's mind to carry him back to an earlier time when he and Kris were little boys, sitting in the corner of their shared bedroom, playing with stuffed animals. He wasn't sure where the game came from, though he supposed it was natural for kids to get lost in the world of make-believe. Their "storylines" were representative of things they saw in their day-to-day life, which left Kyle perplexed by where the fucking culminating every "scene" came from. It wasn't as though they saw people being intimate, and while the act was present in some of the television shows they secretly watched, it was never at the forefront like it was during their game. Regardless of the setup, it didn't take long for Kyle and Kris to have their stuffies simulate sex, and when they did, it was always the same. While Kris was the dominant dog, Kyle was the compliant cat, allowing his kitty to get taken by the horny hound. He couldn't help but question if the power imbalance during play made him crave the upper hand with his brother otherwise, and if the submissive role during the exploration made him wish guys like Luke Larson would save him from big bad bullies before going balls deep in his butt.

It's not that he thought the game made him gay, but he wondered if it had conditioned him at a young age to want to give himself to another person like that rather than be the alpha in the equation. It was so much more appealing to fantasize about somebody taking care of him, showering him with attention, and making him the priority instead of having to put out that effort to do the same for them. He wanted to be coveted, cosseted and chased. He wanted to be wanted in the softest possible ways, like a middle school girl getting notes slid through the slots of her locker by her many admirers. While his friends had wanted to bang her, Kyle had wanted to be her, awash with affection from the guys who thought of him strictly as one of them and not as an object of desire. His mother's rants about his frame often flashed in his head, the message messing him up more than he should have allowed. "Girls won't like you if you're too small," a phrase that never affected him behind his concern that boys wouldn't either. While he knew a lot of guys were into smaller girls, he wondered if they were into smaller guys too. He certainly wasn't. He loved broad chests, muscular arms, hard bodies, and soft smiles. If he was into guys like that, why would any dude be into him? Why did he care? It would be easier if he didn't. He could go about his business, not worried that something was wrong with him.

Shimmying his phone out of the pocket of his skinny jeans, Kyle rested it on his lap, careful not to let the hawk-eyed Ms. Carson catch him texting in class.

Kyle (10:23am): What are you doing?

Richard (10:24am): Trying to pay attention in class.

Kyle (10:24am): Overrated.

Richard (10:25am): What's overrated? School?

Kyle (10:25am): School, paying, and attention.

Richard (10:26am): So are you on your way to becoming a homeless, klepto recluse?

Kyle (10:26am): Maybe. It sounds better than being the loser new kid.

Richard (10:27am): You're still having a hard time fitting in?

Kyle (10:27am): Eh. I'm working an angle, but I don't care as much about friends as I do funds.

Richard (10:27am): Do I even want to know?

Kyle (10:28am): Probably not.

Richard (10:28am): Great.

Kyle (10:29am): Are you talking to anyone?

Richard (10:29am): I'm talking to you right now even though I'm supposed to be paying attention in English.

Kyle (10:30am): I mean hooking up, dating, whatever.

Richard (10:30am): You do remember who you're talking to, don't you?

Kyle laughed, drawing a surly stare from his teacher. Clearing his throat, he shoved his phone back into his pocket and attempted to focus on the boring lecture. Maybe Richard wasn't the best person to talk to about the confusion Kyle was dealing with. While Kris and Matt had an anemic amount of game, Richard's was thinner. Still, Richard's lack of game and the fact that he didn't seem interested in actively seeking out anyone made Kyle feel better about his solo status. He knew holding himself up against an asexual introvert wasn't the fairest comparison, but it settled Kyle's anxiety, at least temporarily. There was something calming in solitude when he was willing to believe it was a prize rather than a curse.

Kyle (10:35am): You don't want someone?

Richard (10:36am): Someone or the right one?

Kyle (10:36am): Either way.

Richard (10:37am): They're nothing alike. One is settling and the other is striving. I don't think I want either though. There's no use differentiating, but I figured it may matter to you.

Kyle (10:38am): Deep. Have you tried not overthinking things and just existing?

Richard (10:38am): That's my daily activity.

Kyle (10:38am): And?

Richard (10:39am): And what?

Kyle (10:39am): How's it going?

Richard (10:39am): I'm here.

Kyle (10:40am): I'm not.

It wasn't lost on him that Richard was living in the town Kyle wished he'd never been forced to leave. As far as Kyle was concerned, his friend was the lucky one.

Richard (10:41am): I meant here in a general way. Like a part of this lonely feeling.

Kyle (10:41am): You get lonely?

Richard (10:43am): I don't know. Maybe I'm just curious about what it would be like to want to be with someone. Shouldn't I want to be? Not craving that makes me feel lonely too.

Kyle (10:43am): At least if you don't want someone, it doesn't hurt when they don't want you back.

Richard (10:44am): It sounds like you have a crush on someone.

Kyle (10:44am): Not really, but one day I probably will, and they won't be into me.

Richard (10:45am): Why do you say that?

Kyle (10:45am): A lot of reasons that I can't get into right now. The bell's about to ring.

Richard (10:46am): I'm glad I could get you through class. I'm looking forward to tomorrow when I fail the quiz I have to take on today's lecture.

Kyle (10:46am): You never fail anything.

The ding of the bell prompted Kyle to rise from his seat and make his way into the busy hallway. He expected to weave through the crowd anonymously, as he typically did, and was surprised when a hand grabbed his wrist.

"Hey, are you that guy?" the tall, thin brunet asked quickly, glancing over his shoulder as if he was being followed.

"Which guy?"

"The weed guy," he replied. "I'm looking to score a dime bag."

"Oh, yeah, that's me," Kyle nodded. Despite the fact that he'd been approached at least once a day for the three weeks they'd been selling, it still took him by surprise when someone knew who he was.

"Do you have anything on you?"

"No, but you can come over to my house after school and I'll get you set up with something."

"Cool, cool." He took his phone out and handed it to Kyle. "Put your number in and I'll text you for the address."

Kyle typed in his digits and handed the iPhone back to the boy.

"Kyle," he said as he looked over the entry in his phone. "I'm Jared."

"Alright," Kyle nodded, trying not to focus on how cute his new customer was. There was something about Jared's energy that made Kyle think they had some things other than weed in common. "See you later."

"Later," Jared confirmed.

Though his back was to Jared as he walked away, Kyle knew the other guy was watching him. And he liked it.

8

Kyle should have expected that shit would go wrong as soon as he replied to Jared's text later that afternoon. His brothers had gotten their dumb asses tossed in detention, and though work on the basement was in full swing, Kyle was pleased to find that there were no contractors in sight. It was an admittedly mundane drug transaction, but for Kyle it was the first thing—besides meaningless glances with Luke in the hallway—he'd looked forward to in Tennessee.

Something about Jared was interesting. He seemed different than the other boys in their school, and while he wasn't necessarily Kyle's type, Kyle actually believed there was a chance that he could be Jared's. The way Jared's blue eyes had regarded Kyle's body had made him feel like he was enough to look at, a train of thought that was foreign to him after years focused on the inadequacy of his frame.

Kyle was packing his after-school bowl on the basement couch when the unwelcome visual of his mother, Lou the contractor, and two men in paint splattered clothes descending the stairs intruded on his ready-to-be-cleared mind.

"Why are they here?" Kyle asked, tucking the pipe and baggie between the cushions as discreetly as possible.

"I don't know if you noticed, but we're in the middle of renovations," Hope replied, clearly unimpressed by Kyle's question. "And we're on a tight timetable."

"A tight timetable that's been dictated by you," Kyle clarified.

Hope bristled, running her fingers through her shoulder-length blonde locks. "What's wrong with some fervor behind it? Are you going to fault me for that too? That I want this too much for you?"

Rolling his eyes, Kyle observed the painters as they poured the weed-green paint he'd chosen for his new bedroom into a tray.

"What?" his mother prodded. It seemed she was itching for a fight as much as he didn't want one.

Reaching for the television remote, Kyle aimlessly clicked through the channels, pretending to be engaged in the search for a show to zone out on. His knee bounced nervously as he considered what to do about Jared. The last thing Kyle wanted to do was tell Jared to come another time. Dealers couldn't be absent. It was too easy for their clients to find another avenue. Besides, Kyle wanted to see him again—to really see him, away from the unforgiving fluorescent lights of the school hallway. It wasn't a matter of attraction; it was obvious that Jared was a good-looking guy. It was more of a hope that a softer light would allow Jared to show a side of himself that Kyle already presumed to know. The thought of accepting his nature had intimidated Kyle in Texas, but the thought of doing so in Tennessee felt like a death wish. Iris Valley was as backwoods as it got, a factory line of fag bashing, and nowhere near the kind of place he'd be comfortable exploring his inclinations. Jared's apparent confidence in who he was was even more impressive given the hostile environment. While he wasn't flamboyant, he also didn't seem scared, and that was something of significance. Kyle wasn't sure if he was interested in Jared or envious of him. There was a freedom in transparency that Kyle doubted he would achieve. He figured that instead of perseverating over his inadequacy, he should focus his attention to more pressing matters.

When Hope sat down beside him on the sofa, Kyle couldn't help himself, ready to sink his teeth into the argument she was seemingly angling for.

"Why are *you* here?" Kyle asked, rephrasing his prior question to reflect the intent.

"I live here," Hope reminded, shaking her head in exasperation.

"Since when?"

"You know," she sighed, "I didn't raise you to be so rude."

"Maybe it was the nannies then," Kyle offered, unwilling to temper his snark. "They did most of the heavy lifting, right?"

"Now you fault me for having a successful career?" Hope asked, standing up and beginning to pace the room. "Can you name one time when you didn't get what you wanted, Kyle? You pointed to a toy and had it within the day."

Can you name one time when you didn't get what you wanted? It was a loaded question. Kyle could recall plenty of times when she didn't give him what he wanted. While his mother always came through with the toys and treats, the attention he truly craved was less generously provided. In the past, he'd tried to explain the differentiation to Hope, but somehow when the subject was raised, his astute mother immediately became obtuse. It was as if she couldn't fathom that she'd somehow sacrificed a deeper connection with her children for a high-power career. He wondered if she would have been more likely to acknowledge it, and be less defensive, if she hadn't lost her job—if everything had been worth it in a way.

Kyle vividly remembered the day his mother told him and his brothers she had been laid off. It was a midsummer afternoon, and he was sitting on the driveway, tinkering with the busted chain on his bicycle. The Texas sage that lined the asphalt was in full bloom and he was glad the house looked especially nice for his and Kris' fourteenth birthday bash that weekend. Summer parties typically had a lower-than-average turnout, but theirs were never plagued by a reduced number of revelers. Their birthdays were so epic that Kyle was pretty positive families planned their vacations around the date. Hope and Ken loved to party, and they passed their sociability genes down to Kyle and Kris. While Matt partook in the fun, he was never as invested as the rest of the Rosses were.

Kyle hadn't expected to see his mom's Lincoln Navigator pulling into the driveway at that time of day. He watched as she parked her car, blotting the corners of her eyes with an overworked tissue when she stepped out to face him. He hadn't fully understood the implications of the news, hadn't comprehended how much of an impact that moment would have on the following years. He was happy, thinking that her increased freedom would mean there was more time for them to spend together. Instead, he'd gotten a half-assed birthday party, divorced parents, an unmotivated mother, and a one-way ticket to Tennessee. Due to her inability to channel the quality of her name, Hope was never the same, so none of them were.

"Are you sure about that green?" Hope questioned from where she was now standing beside the doorframe of Kyle's future bedroom. He sighed at her insistence to bring his thoughts back to the basement and another sign of her disapproval. The grimace on her face made it obvious she wasn't crazy about the color.

"I love it," Kyle decided, his confidence surging with every apprehensive glance she gave the walls. "It's perfect."

A soft knock on the back door cut off his mother's retort.

"Who's that?" Hope asked as Kyle crossed the basement to open up.

"Don't worry about it," Kyle replied, purposely avoiding eye contact with Jared. "Come in." Sliding his hands into his pockets, Kyle nodded toward the stairway, "Uh, we can go upstairs and study. It's unexpectedly loud down here."

Jared appeared to be confused for a moment before a look that confirmed cognition flashed across his face. "Sounds good."

"Are you going to introduce me to your friend?" Hope asked, already approaching Jared, hand outstretched.

His friend. Maybe Jared could be. Of all the people he'd met in Tennessee, a friendship with Jared seemed the most likely. Since he had so many friends in Texas, Kyle had never craved platonic companionship as much as he did a physical connection, but his loneliness in Iris Valley had flipped the script, making it nearly impossible to want anything more than he wanted inclusion.

"It's nice to meet you ma'am," Jared said with a smile so warm it almost made it easy for Kyle to forget he was in the basement for business—easy to believe there could possibly be something to build between them. He chided himself for getting wrapped up in unlikely possibilities but knew the admonishment couldn't kill the modicum of optimism he was able to muster. It felt good to think the best for a change.

Hope seemed charmed, which made her next action even more confusing. As Jared tended to his ringing phone, Hope caught the contractor's attention and held her arm up, very purposely displaying a limp wrist. The contractor nodded his agreement as Kyle stood shocked in his spot. It wasn't like he and his brothers didn't throw around derogatory terms daily, but it felt different when it came from his mother, more pointed. She should have known better. She was supposed to *be* better than them. Jared hadn't done anything but walk into the room, comfortable in his lanky body and unabashed by the slightly effeminate quality of his voice.

Hope's reaction to Jared made Kyle like him more, while simultaneously wanting him to get the fuck out of his house. If Hope felt she had a good read on a stranger, how was it she lacked the ability to identify the telling qualities of her own son. Perhaps she didn't, but she never talked about it. Maybe she knew more about Kyle than he believed she did, things that he wasn't ready for anyone to know, that he barely admitted to himself. He couldn't wait until the renovations were done so he could go back to sporadically seeing her when a sliver of guilt dragged her back into the mix. And as he led Jared up to his bedroom to handle the transaction, Kyle hoped that one day her guilt would consume her, for more betrayals than just one.

9

Though Kyle would never admit it to his mother, the basement was pretty sweet once it was done. Not only did it feel like an apartment completely unconnected from the mostly abandoned top floors, but it was also chill as fuck. As infrequently as their mother stepped foot in the house, she peeked into the basement even less. The privacy allowed Kyle and his brothers to sell a shit-ton of weed and hang out with customers who were quickly turning into friends. It was crazy how popular guys could become when they had an endless supply of weed and unprecedented freedom. The Ross house was the place to be, and it seemed people were paying just to party, less concerned about the cost and quality of the weed than Kyle had expected. They were selling an experience, and their classmates were eagerly tossing cash to be a part of it.

Despite his surge in popularity, Kyle still struggled to feel like he belonged where he didn't want to be in the first place. As much as it sucked to be stuck in Iris Valley, it was much easier to cope with his displacement when people were trying to be his pal rather than pick on him. It barely mattered that their intentions weren't pure. After all, his weren't either.

"This is the life," Kris grinned, draping his arm over Kyle's shoulder.

Kyle nodded, watching as people he barely recognized streamed into the basement. A few weeks earlier, he would've never imagined their house would be the go-to party place. While he'd grown used to the afternoon bunch showing up to get high and buy weed, he never thought any of them would want to hang out beyond the transaction, especially since they weren't providing anyone with anything free. In fact, the partiers brought their own beer and were more than happy to share whatever they had with their de facto hosts. It was the first sign of Southern hospitality Kyle had experienced since moving months before, and though he'd never admit it aloud, he kind of liked it.

"It would be," Kyle said, resting his head on his twin's shoulder.

Kris sighed. "You have to move on. Everyone's sick of hearing you complain about how much you hate it here."

Clicking his tongue, Kyle replied: "I mean, I still hate it here, but I meant it 'would be' the life if you sat your ass down on the couch and packed me a bowl."

"Wait," Kris said, pulling back so he could gape at Kyle overdramatically. "Are you actually taking the night off from your incessant complaining?"

"I don't complain that much," Kyle disagreed, laughing as Kris continued to ham up his reaction. "Fuck off, nerd."

Unfazed, Kris yawned. "Speaking of nerds, have you talked to Richard lately?"

Kyle nodded. "We text and stuff."

"How's he surviving without you?"

Rolling his eyes, Kyle flicked his brother's ear. "Jealous bitch."

"Like I give a shit," Kris tsked.

Regardless of how much Kris tried to play it off, Kyle knew he most certainly did give a shit. They both did. It had to be some weird twin thing, but there was always the semblance of a threat when friends got too close. It was as if they thought they could be replaced, even though Kyle knew what they had was irreplaceable. There was something powerful about sharing a source of life with someone, especially when it had nourished you at the same time.

"Hey Texas," a guy Kyle recognized from Physics class called to him from the couch, where he was lounging with his arms draped around the shoulders of the two hot girls sitting beside him. "Come here."

For a moment, Kyle wasn't sure if he was talking to him or Kris, but his brother gently pushing him forward made it clear.

"What's up?" Kyle asked, dipping his hands into the pockets of his jeans as he approached the couch.

"Hang on," he said, letting go of the girls so he could shift and get a joint out of his wallet. "Share this with me."

"Why?" Kyle wondered, perplexed by the act of kindness. While he didn't have issues with anyone at Iris Valley High School, people didn't typically go out of their way to endear themselves to him, even with his newfound notoriety. He sat on the edge of coffee table and regarded the guy tentatively.

"I'm in Physics with you," he replied. "Brian, remember?"

Brian said his name in a way that alluded to the fact that he had taken the time to introduce himself months before. He hadn't.

"Uh, no," Kyle said, shaking his head a bit to get the blond locks lying on his forehead off of his face.

Brian laughed. "Wow, Texas, you're embarrassing me in front of these ladies. They're going to think I'm not in with the cool kids."

"Cool kids?" Kyle scoffed, glancing around at all the people packed into his basement. Maybe over the course of the last several weeks that was exactly who he'd become—a cool kid. Maybe he was actually the guy who had impromptu parties that people wanted to attend. Maybe he'd unknowingly achieved a social standing similar to that which he had enjoyed in Texas. Maybe it had all happened exactly when he'd stopped giving a shit, but maybe he still didn't. He didn't want to fit in, he wanted to get out.

"I mean," Brian began with a shrug, "yeah. You live in a big house and you have the whole basement to yourself."

"I share it with my brothers," Kyle corrected.

One of the girls laughed. "Does that even matter? You have, like, total freedom down here." She curled her long red hair around her slim index finger. "It's awesome."

"Really awesome," the other girl agreed, licking her full lips. "You probably have a lot of company, right?"

Kyle didn't respond. Instead, he held a hand up to present the crowded room.

"I meant personal company," she clarified.

"Like bedroom company," the redhead added. "You must have a lot of bedroom company."

The girls giggled in a way that Kyle thought only happened in the movies and Brian sighed, smoothing his flyaways down as he lit the joint. "You guys are laying it on thick, aren't you?" he muttered, his voice teeming with jealousy. "Are you smoking, Texas?"

Kyle nodded, holding his hand out to take the joint from Brian. As he inhaled, he grinned. "This is my shit, huh? Either mine or Johnny's...and you seem like a smart guy so it has to be mine."

"It's one and the same," Brian smirked. "You have quite the monopoly going in Iris Valley. You're going to put Johnny out of business."

"Not a chance," Kyle disagreed. "He gets paid before we do. He has margins. Don't worry at all about him."

"I'm not worried," the redhead interjected. "I think it's super hot that you're such an astute businessman."

"I think it's hot that you know the word 'astute,'" Brian told her, looking at her breasts lecherously.

"Is it because I have tits that you think I'm dumb?" she bristled, glaring at Brian for a moment before standing up and straightening her miniskirt. "It was nice to meet you, Texas," she said to Kyle, giving him a flirty wink.

"It's Kyle," he stated before taking another drag of the joint. Out of the corner of his eye, he could see her checking him out, but he made a conscious decision not to return the gaze.

"I'm Emma," she said, holding her hand out so it crossed his line of vision.

Politely, he turned his head and shook her hand. It was impossible not to notice the way her almond-shaped, green eyes sparkled thanks to the attention. She was pretty, with her pale, freckled skin and pouty lips, narrow waist, and slender hips. He should have cared that she was showing interest, but he couldn't force himself to give a shit.

"Emmalynn," the brunette interjected. "Don't try to shake off the Tennessee all of a sudden, Em."

Emma gave her friend the finger, as her cheeks flushed pink.

"It's nice to meet you, Emma," Kyle stated purposefully.

"You've got some game, Texas," Brian complimented. "Players recognize players, you know what I mean?"

"I actually don't," Kyle replied.

The conversation had long since run its course and all he wanted to do was lay down on his bed, stare up at the ceiling, and chill. Suddenly, the basement being inhabited by randoms was awfully inconvenient, and regardless of how lucrative he knew their presence would be in the long run, Kyle wished they were gone.

"I'm gonna go," Kyle said, standing up abruptly. He heard Brian spouting some pleasantries as he walked away, but they were muffled by the din of voices from every direction. Surveying the room, Kyle attempted to find a familiar face, preferably one belonging to one of his brothers. When he saw Jared leaning against the wall sipping a bottle of beer, Kyle smiled. Although they hadn't hung out aside from the routine smoking session that followed a purchase, he felt comfortable with him.

"Hey," he greeted, grabbing Jared's elbow and nodding his head toward his bedroom. "Wanna chill?"

"Yeah, okay," Jared grinned, following Kyle's lead.

A fingertip gently tickling the dip of his lower back told Kyle that Jared knew what was going down. Snaps and surges of energy pulsed through his excited body. It had been too long since he'd been touched like that. He needed to be held, kissed, fucked. It might have been risky to hook up when half of the school was hanging out just beyond the walls, but the weed persuaded Kyle not to worry.

Upon opening his bedroom door, Kyle found a couple making out on the bed, shirts twisted as they rolled on his comforter. "Out," he ordered, tapping the dude on the shoulder. "C'mon."

The duo looked up at Kyle wide-eyed and mumbled their apologies before scurrying from the space.

As soon as the lock latched, Jared caught Kyle's lips. The kiss was a fervent assurance that Jared wanted to kiss him as badly as he wanted to be kissed. Hands traveled over bodies as they tumbled to the bed, frantically stripping their clothes off while their mouths struggled to stay connected. The hum of the party a few feet away from them somehow made the whole scene sexier to Kyle. Though he certainly didn't want anyone to find out he was fucking around with a guy, the act of sneaking to do so had him particularly aroused.

Kyle moaned his approval as he rubbed the big bulge in Jared's black pants. "Nice."

Breathless, Jared peeled their lips apart, gazing down at Kyle with blown-out pupils, "I'm not gay."

"You're what?" Kyle whispered, confused by the admission.

"I'm *not* gay," he repeated deliberately.

"Your hand is on my dick."

"Yours is on mine too," Jared pointed out. "Does that make you..." he paused for long enough to get cut off by an irritated Kyle:

"Horny."

"Right," Jared agreed, leaning in for another kiss.

The only Tennessean Kyle had identified as a guy who owned who he was and seemed relatively proud of that person was anything but. It would have been more disheartening if Kyle's heart was in it, but he'd left it behind in Texas months ago. Seeing as though Kyle was confused enough about his own sexual identity, he had no desire to embark on a conversation about labels and semantics. Instead, he laid back while the "straight" guy fucked him like a faggot.

10

Emma was nice, and it was her sweetness that made the concept of having a girlfriend feel alright to Kyle. That and the fact that their relationship had come about in an organic way. It started with Emma seeking Kyle out in the cafeteria. While he no longer sat alone, he always positioned himself at the end of the table, an easy out if his company became too annoying. Kyle could only endure so much talk about trucks and football. He wondered why none of the jocks coveted exotics the way he did. Were they really so brainwashed by the boondocks that they couldn't even fathom owning the better things in life?

The first time Emma took the seat across from Kyle, the guys had a field day with their wolf whistles and comments. Evidently, Emma was pretty popular thanks to her post as the captain of the cheer squad. Though he wasn't attracted to her, Kyle liked the attention he got from their connection. Every glance and giggle they garnered felt like a "fuck you" to his mother, who was so convinced no girl would ever want his skinny ass. Emma wanted it—bad. In fact, her desire to get dicked down was the worst part of their budding relationship. Making out was fine, but Kyle definitely didn't want to bang. He tried to reason that a hole was a hole, but it wasn't just a hole when it was a vagina—it was lips and drips and he couldn't have been less interested in exploring the clammy cave.

"Deeper," Emma whispered as Kyle tentatively traced his fingertip around her opening. "Push them in deeper."

He'd heard her the first time, but was having difficulty finagling his fingers deeper into the wetness. Why was she so wet? Theoretically he knew it was because she was turned on, but how could she be finding the hookup so hot when he wasn't into at all? It was as though they were on completely different planes, touching each other through a film that filtered out any possible pleasure.

Sighing into Emma's hungry mouth as he dragged his tongue along her bottom teeth, Kyle shoved his digits in all the way to the knuckle and squeezed his eyes shut at the sound of her moan. As he fingered Emma, he thought of his mother and how she doubted that he'd ever get a girl. The joke was on her. His newfound popularity at Iris Valley ensured that he could pull plenty of pussy, but it was becoming increasingly obvious to him, no matter how hard he tried to fight it, that he would much rather play with a penis than a pretty girl's puss.

"C'mon, deeper," she urged. "Add a finger."

Kyle did as he was told, trying not to be concerned that he would perforate an organ with the rhythmic jabbing. No matter how much he gave her, she demanded more.

"I want you inside me," Emma whispered, her breath hot and wet on Kyle's neck.

"I am inside you," Kyle said breathlessly, exhausted by the physical and mental exertion it took to continue the hookup.

"Your dick," she laughed, moving her hand to the crotch of his jeans. Pulling her lips off of his skin, she sat up straight and stared at him with confusion clouding her face. "You're not hard."

"So?" he bristled, sliding his hand out of her panties and shifting uncomfortably on his bed.

"So...most guys at least get hard when they're fingering a girl. Is there something wrong with me? I mean, did I do something wrong?"

Emma asked nervously. "Something that turned you off or whatever?"

"No," Kyle promised, shaking his head. "It's not like that."

"What's it like then?" she pressed, her tone more concerned than confrontational.

"I smoked a lot before you came over," he said, and while it wasn't a lie, it wasn't the reason for his limp cock. He wished that he could force blood down to his dick, implore it to harden so he could provide Emma with concrete evidence that he wasn't different from other guys she'd been with.

"Oh," she exhaled, nodding her understanding. "Is it always like that?"

"Uh," Kyle sniffed uncomfortably, "not always, but a lot of the time, I guess."

"I'll have to catch you before you're high then," Emma grinned, intertwining her fingers with Kyle's. "Maybe I can skip cheer practice tomorrow and come over right after school..."

It was odd that instead of asking Kyle to take an afternoon off from smoking, Emma wanted to show up to his house earlier in hopes he would be less high.

"It's part of the business model, you know?" Kyle replied dumbly. "I smoke people out and then they buy more weed. I can't just skip it."

"Maybe smoke less then," she suggested. "That way it will wear off by the time I'm done with practice." She loosened her grip on his hand. "Unless you don't really want to do stuff with me." Emma's insecurity was glaring, and Kyle didn't blame her for her self-doubt. He would've felt the same way.

"I'm a guy," he said matter-of-factly. "Of course I want to do stuff."

Because guys wanted to fuck girls. That was what guys did. Kyle's dad had taught them about the birds and the bees at a young age. Kyle knew how it all worked. He just wasn't sure why he never worked right, why he didn't get hard while fingering girls but was a rock when he messed with boys. The easy answer was that he was gay, but the hard part was figuring out how he functioned so disparately from how he was supposed to. Though he rarely had deep conversations about emotions with Kris, Kyle was aware that his twin was into girls. It was obvious in how he drooled over Emma and jacked off to women with tits the size of their heads that Kris was wired the right way—the way they were expected to be. When Kyle called Kris a faggot or queer, he knew there was no truth to the assertion, but he wondered if Kris knew when he gave it back to him that it was exactly who he was. He wanted to be like his brother. They were born the same, genes and blood, but somehow Kyle was different, and no amount of make-out sessions with Emma or interest from other girls was going to change that.

"Lay back," Emma prompted, gently pushing Kyle's chest as an indication that she wanted him reclined. "I'll suck you off."

"Uh, it's alright."

"It's alright?" she repeated, her eyebrows furrowed. "What does that even mean? You don't want me to give you head?"

"I told you, I'm really high. I don't want you to waste your time," he reasoned. It was difficult not to cringe through the words. There was no way Emma would buy that he was too high for a blowjob. Nobody could be that dense. It would only be a matter of moments before she would realize what he was and expose him to the school. His popularity would be as short-lived as any one of Matt's relationships, and his business would be obliterated. Once the easy money that made living in Tennessee an iota more tolerable was gone, he would be too. There was no way he could stay in the backward state and suffer the ramifications of his sexuality.

"It wouldn't be a waste of time," Emma pouted. "I want to."

Kyle gnawed on his lower lip, knowing hordes of dudes would die to sit in his position while he was dying to sit anywhere else.

"I could eat..." he began, shuddering at the thought. The realization that he couldn't muster the nerve to mutter the rest of the offer had Kyle switching up his approach. "I could eat a whole fucking pizza right now."

Emma stared at him for a beat, her mouth slowly allowing a gleaming smile to take over. "You have the munchies, huh?"

"Something wicked," he confirmed, grinning back. "I'll give you a slice."

"Then you wouldn't be eating the whole fucking pizza," she smirked. "You said you could eat the whole thing."

"I'll demolish it," he promised as he stood up, holding his hand out for Emma so he could playfully yank her off the bed. A quick peck on the lips had his girlfriend glowing and Kyle feeling relieved.

"I don't know where you put it all," she teased, rubbing a hand over his taut stomach. "If I ate a whole pizza, it would end up on my ass and thighs."

"You're perfect."

Emma visibly melted into a pile of mush as Kyle led her out to the driveway where her car was parked.

The car ride was quiet in a comfortable and companionable way. Though it was obvious Emma wanted more, it was good to have a friend Kyle could feel comfortable with. Things were okay with Jared; their relationship hadn't progressed at all, which was what Kyle expected after realizing how repressed Jared was. With Emma it was easier, even when she tried to mount him.

"I love this song," she announced, beginning to sing along to the music on the radio.

Once Emma was sufficiently distracted, Kyle got his phone out of his pocket and shot off a text to Richard.

Kyle (9:23pm): I'm with my girlfriend right now.

Richard (9:25pm): Girlfriend? That's new.

Kyle (9:25pm): Yeah. She's cool.

Richard (9:26pm): That's cool.

Kyle (9:27pm): I don't know. It's kinda dumb.

Richard (9:27pm): Did you just call your girlfriend "it"?

Kyle (9:28pm): LOL no. She's not an "it" and she's not dumb. The whole girlfriend thing is dumb.

Richard (9:28pm): Why's it dumb?

Kyle's palms began to sweat as he stared down at the phone screen, debating if he should type what was on his mind. He needed to try it, to see how it felt. If worst came to worst, Richard would stop talking to him. Until recently, their correspondences had been sporadic at best. Kyle could handle the blow if he had to.

Kyle (9:31pm): I don't like girls like that.

Richard (9:31pm): Then why are you with one?

With his hands shaking, Kyle attempted to process Richard's lack of shock. It hadn't even been thirty seconds since his admission, and his friend had responded seemingly unfazed.

Kyle (9:32pm): That's it?

Richard (9:32pm): What do you mean?

Kyle (9:32pm): You acted like I just said the sky was blue.

Richard (9:33pm): A statement just as obvious as the last one you made.

Kyle (9:33pm): Really?

He didn't know whether to be relieved or insulted.

Richard (9:33pm): Yeah.

Richard (9:33pm): You know what else?

Kyle (9:34pm): What?

Richard (9:34pm): I don't like them either.

And with that, neither of them was shocked.

11

Richard's acceptance would have been wonderful if they actually lived close enough to one another for it to matter. Kyle had been sure he would be able to get past the blow of his friend not accepting the fact that he was gay and, unfortunately, he found it easy to get past the initial relief. Richard was hundreds of miles away, and Kyle was in Iris Valley on his own. What did it matter if a friend he would probably never see again was cool with his sexuality? Hope had made her predictions regarding long-term friendships with those in Texas abundantly clear. Tennessee was their forever, leaving the Lone Star state to fade away like the memories made there.

Richard's admission that he wasn't into women was about as surprising as the sun rising in the East and setting in the West. Kyle was aware that his friend wasn't interested in men either, and he couldn't help but be envious of Richard's sexual aversion to both sexes. Somehow, it seemed more admissible to be turned off by girls if one was apathetic toward boys too. Kyle wished he wasn't plagued by a penchant for penis. There was no doubt he could've coped with all aspects of his life better if he didn't crave cock. Iris Valley would've even been a more appealing place to live. After all, he had a gorgeous girlfriend and a fair bit of popularity thanks to the booming weed business. Though he would never admit it aloud to his family, things could have been worse. They *had* been worse. But they'd never truly improve as long as he was who he was—*what* he was.

"You look like you have a lot on your mind," Hope noted as Kyle pushed a sausage link around his plate. "Anything you want to talk about?"

"Nope," Kyle replied coolly, avoiding eye contact with the intruder.

Obviously getting the hint that Kyle was disinterested in looking at her during the discussion,

Hope made her way over to the sink. "I saw Emma leaving while I was pulling up. Did she stay the night?"

"Yup."

"We're allowed to have girls sleep over now?" Matt questioned, clicking his tongue. "That's new."

"Emma's here every night so it's not new," Kris interjected. "You could have a girl stay over too if you could ever, you know, get a girl."

Kris and Kyle laughed as Matt pursed his lips, unamused.

"Wow," their older brother nodded. "I guess it's a free-for-all around here."

"Again, not really new," Kris stated, taking a bite of his toast.

"Is it so wrong to trust you guys?" Hope asked as she washed one of the many dirty dishes that had been waiting for her. "Should I not be proud that I raised such responsible children?"

Kyle couldn't help but guffaw at how dense his mother was, especially regarding the criminal activity going on under her roof. It served her right for never being around and, despite the inconvenient illegality of the weed business, they were serving the community. The vibe at IVHS was much better than it had been at the beginning of the school year. They were keeping the student body high and happy.

Hope wiped her hands on a dish towel that had been lying on the cluttered counter and faced her sons. "Am I wrong to trust you?" she repeated, her eyebrows raised high.

"Not at all," Kris promised, ever the eager mama's boy. "You can trust us just fine, Ma."

Matt indiscreetly masked an accusatory "liar" with a cough, drawing an irritated glare from Kris and a chuckle from Kyle.

"I'm not stupid," Hope stated, grabbing her keys from the edge of the island. "I know you aren't angels. You're teenagers, for goodness' sake, but I'm not getting calls from your school or from the police, so I'm willing to call that a win."

"Winner, winner, the 'best beans you've ever tasted' for dinner," Matt said, slinging his backpack over his shoulder. "Are we going or what?"

"Since when are you in a rush to get to school?" Kris asked, narrowing his eyes as if he was searching Matt's face for a tell.

"Since today," Matt replied.

The vagueness should have prompted Kyle to question the reason as well, but he had other things on his mind. "Walk with me today," he urged Kris as they lit their Newports on the porch.

"Why the hell would I do that?" Kris scoffed, cupping his hand to protect the flame from the balmy fall breeze.

"Because I want you to," Kyle answered flatly, blowing a plume of smoke in Kris' direction.

"It's not something you want to share with the class?" Matt asked, glancing up from where he was crouched to tie his shoe.

"I know that you've piqued *my* interest," Hope added, much to Kyle's chagrin.

"So, are you walking with me or what?" Kyle pressed, trying to relay the importance of the conversation to Kris via twin telepathy.

"I guess I'm walking with you," Kris relented, following Kyle down the stairs.

"I guess I'm riding with Mom," Matt called after them, his tone hinting at the jealousy Kyle knew he was riddled with.

The three of them were so close in age that it made it obvious how far apart Matt was from Kris and Kyle. Their older brother had been too young to remember life without them, and Kyle and Kris had lived their lives as if they only needed each other. A brotherly bond paled in comparison to the intensity of a twin connection. Any other siblings born in such a slim succession would be inseparable, but it was clear it had been hard for Matt to suction himself to them even when he'd tried.

"I've been thinking about your idea," Kyle began once they reached the end of the driveway, far from earshot.

"Which one?" Kris wondered, lifting an interested eyebrow. "Are you good with me pretending to be you so I can plow Emma? Because that's no doubt my best and brightest."

Kyle laughed, not only because his brother was a clever bastard, but because it was hilarious that Kris actually believed he and Emma were having sex. Of course, it made sense for Kris to jump to that conclusion, but the truth was significantly more PG. Somehow—once his weed-related excuses had been exhausted—Kyle successfully convinced his girlfriend that he was asexual. And when she'd asked why he wanted to be with her at all, he'd given the most Richard response he could come up with: companionship.

"Is that it?" Kris asked hopefully. "You want me to bang your girl? You need a night off?"

"Try again," Kyle chuckled.

"I literally can't think of anything right now besides fucking Emma," Kris admitted with a smirk.

"What about Xanax? Can you think about that?"

"Still Emma, but Xanax is a solid attempt at diversion."

"Remember when you suggested we sell off some of mom's stock?" Kyle continued. "I think we should do it."

Kris halted on the rocky pavement to stare at Kyle, surprised. "Oh yeah?"

"Mm-hmm," Kyle nodded, tapping his cigarette and watching as the glowing embers flitted in the space between them.

"I thought you weren't about diversifying."

"Well, I changed my mind," Kyle said easily, beginning to walk again. "C'mon, we're going to be late if you just stand there gawking at me."

"Since when do you care about being late to school?"

Kyle lifted his arms over his head and dipped his head back to look at the cerulean sky. "Change is in the air, man. Don't you feel it?"

"Obviously not like you do, but I'm down to make some real money," Kris replied, keeping up with Kyle's strides.

"Do you have any idea how many of her vials are full?"

"I haven't counted, but several."

"How is she able to hoard them? I mean, she's clearly not taking it..."

Unlike Kris, Kyle made it a point *not* to keep up with Hope's bullshit. He wasn't sure why his twin felt so compelled to be a support system for someone who never supported them, but he continuously put forth the effort.

"No. She takes it. It's just that every time a therapist tells her something she doesn't like, she switches to new one and gets another script."

"So basically the therapists tell her she's a cunt and then she bounces," Kyle scoffed, rolling his eyes. "Sounds about right."

"You're too hard on her," Kris tsked, a refrain of his typical Captain-Save-a-Hope mantra. "Seriously, she's trying. She tricked out the basement for us."

"She banished us to the basement," Kyle corrected, "and it's hardly 'tricked out.' The bathroom doesn't even have a fucking toilet. You're too easy on her."

"I don't know about that," Kris disagreed. "Either way, I'm into selling the pills. We're going to make a mint."

"How much do they go for per pill?"

"From what I understand, the market isn't saturated at all. We could probably pull in two bucks a pill, so a bottle with ninety in it would be..."

"A hundred and eighty," Kyle grinned.

"I could've done that math. It's not hard math," Kris pouted.

"Right, but I did it faster."

"It's elementary school math."

"That's why you should've been faster," Kyle snarked.

"I had to swallow. Like, I was talking and I had to take a breath and swallow."

"You could've done that after you did the easy math."

"Now you're going to tell me when I can breathe, you bossy little bitch?" Kris sighed. "You really should let me screw your woman. It's only fair."

"You're kinda pathetic," Kyle chided, finding it oddly awesome that Kris was envious of his relationship. While Kyle never cared much when his brothers had girlfriends, he did feel pangs of jealousy, not because he wanted a girlfriend of his own, but because of how simple it was for them to be who they were and get praised for it. It was a foreign concept for him, and one he wanted to grasp.

"You won't be saying that when I get the Xanny business off the ground," Kris promised with a wink. "You'll be eating your words."

"How 'bout you eat my ass," Kyle retorted, giving his brother's butt a smack.

"Fucking fag," Kris laughed, as he ran from the next slap.

Maybe so, but he was about to be a rich one.

12

Kyle figured it would be irresponsible to peddle pills if he didn't sample them first. From what he knew about Xanax prior to giving it a try, he didn't think it had much of an effect on people. After all, his mother was still fucked up and she'd been on the drug forever. If it had been effective, maybe she would have been as well. Either way, when the initial pill didn't do anything but make him a little sleepy, Kyle wasn't surprised. He could have continued to take the medication in hopes it would have gotten him high, but it seemed like a waste of time.

Kyle's complaints were met with Kris' explanation about how users had to let it "build in their systems." He reiterated that the slow rise would ensure they'd have committed customers who would continue to come back for more, and while Kyle understood the model, he wished for his sake that the Xanax would hit harder. Weed was great but having easy access to something stronger wouldn't be a bad way to get through the remainder of the school year.

Compelled to understand what all the rage was about, Kyle decided to consult Google and was instantly informed that he was going about things all wrong. He should have considered that, like any pill, the Xanax could be crushed and delivered directly into his bloodstream via his nose. All it took was one fat line for Kyle to concede that Xanax was a really fucking good time. All his worries about Tennessee, his mother, his sexuality, and his body were washed away by a powerful wave of euphoria. Everything that mattered before didn't matter anymore and he smiled at the thought that it may never matter again. He was matter, solid and liquid, particles of a person pieced together, no heart or head. No worries.

"What do you think?" Kris asked, dabbing his nostril with his knuckle.

"I'm not thinking at all," Kyle grinned.

"So now you see what all the hype is about."

"One hundred percent. I'm kind of second-guessing selling it though."

Kris crinkled his nose with confusion. "What?"

"We should keep it all for ourselves," Kyle said, the statement laced with more truth than he would have liked. Selling weed was a business. It was the means to a very specific end, and while he enjoyed getting high, he prioritized making money. The moment he caught himself slipping into complacency, he recalibrated and reprioritized—something he feared he wouldn't be able to do with Xanax. The drug was mind-numbing in the most liberating way.

"Ha ha ha," Kris punched out sarcastically. "We're doubling our profits by selling it. I know you. You're not going to turn that cash down for a little fun."

"Duh," Kyle agreed, wishing he didn't feel the pull to do just that. He picked up the vial and rolled it in his hands, enjoying the sound of the pills clanking against the plastic. "This shit is our ticket out of here."

"Why do you want to get out so bad anyway?" Kris asked, crossing his arms over his chest and sinking deeper into the overstuffed couch. "I understood it before, but things are pretty good now, right? You're probably as popular here as you were at West River and you have Emma. I'd have thought the urgency to be back in Texas would've waned."

It was a fair assumption, but Kris' blasé attitude only served to confirm what Kyle had already thought—Kris was never as affected by the uprooting as Kyle had been. In the beginning, Kyle theorized that Kris' loyalty to Hope had inspired his twin to bury his actual feelings about the move, but as time ticked on, it became clearer that Kris just wasn't as fazed. Though he'd never admitted anything of the sort, Kyle wondered if his twin had appreciated the fresh start and the fact that he had been able to fit in better than Kyle had. While Kris certainly wasn't an outcast at West River, his low-key vibe ensured that he often took a back seat to Kyle's gregarious personality.

It was strange to consider how intensely his outlook on just about everything changed as soon as his mother announced the move. None of the events after Hope's layoff had come as a shock to him. Though his parents' divorce had sucked, the relentless fighting leading up to it had eradicated any doubt that a breakup was on the horizon. The inevitability hadn't made it any easier to deal with, but nothing was more difficult than Tennessee. It was a betrayal. Hope had pulled them away from the kids they grew up with two years before graduation and forced them into a school, and town, where they didn't fit in so she could be with a guy who wasn't their father. Kyle couldn't understand how his brothers had been able to get past any of it.

"My urgency to go back to Texas will never wane," Kyle promised. "There might be nothing waiting for us when we get back there, but it will still be better than here. Anywhere is better than here."

"Because it's Iris Valley, or does it represent more than that to you?"

"What do you think?" Kyle questioned, pulling his knees to his chest and wrapping his arms around his legs. Even though it was Kris asking the questions, Kyle felt vulnerable from the exposure. He fought his initial impulse to attack, instead deciding to turn things around on his twin. It seemed like he had it all figured out anyway.

"I think it's more than this bumfuck town," Kris answered. "I think if you start to like it here it'll be like Mom won. You'd never let that happen. You'll make yourself miserable to spite her, even if it impacts you negatively too. The moment you let up on the hate, she can breathe. You don't want that."

"So I'm suffocating Mom with my misery?" Kyle smirked. "That's a new one. How long did it take you to conjure up that level of bullshit?"

Kris laughed. "What am I, a wizard? Conjure? Who conjures things? If I could do that, I sure as hell wouldn't be focused on conjuring bullshit."

"What would you conjure then?" Kyle asked with a yawn. As much as he didn't want to go down the rabbit hole with Kris, he was happy to distract his brother from his previous line of questioning.

"Hmm. I don't know. I would say a ton of money, but we're doing well and I like that we're earning it. It wouldn't mean as much if it was just given to us."

"You're an idiot!" Kyle exclaimed. "I'll take easy money any day."

"But think about how much we didn't appreciate when we were growing up," Kris continued. "We got anything we wanted so nothing meant much. Now that we have to work for it, it means everything."

"I get taking pride in earning it for ourselves, but who doesn't dream about a fucking windfall. Rich is rich no matter how you get there."

"I don't know. I think it's good to struggle a little bit. If Mom never lost her job, we would've been lazy, spoiled rich kids," Kris reasoned.

"Which would be so much worse than drug dealers," Kyle joked, tickling his brother's side. He persisted as Kris tumbled into hysterics and tried to kick Kyle off of him.

"Quit it, quit it," Kris cried breathlessly from where he was squirming on the floor. "C'mon, stop!"

Deciding to take mercy on Kris before he pissed on the new carpet, Kyle settled back into the couch, fanning his tickling fingers in warning as soon as Kris did the same.

"I'll break your hand."

"Mm-hmm."

Kris' glare was rife with annoyance. "You know what I mean,

douche. Our lives would be too perfect if we always had it all. What would we have struggled with?"

Kyle knew the question was rhetorical, but he could think of plenty. "It is what it is," he sighed. "I know shit could be worse. It was worse before, but I still hate it here. I hate the way it smells. I hate the beans and moonshine. I hate what it represents. I hate everything."

"I get it, you hate it," Kris stated. "Do you ever get tired of complaining?"

"You asked me, I answered. Do you ever get tired of being a dick?"

Kris grinned. "Not really. It comes really natural to me so I just kinda go with it. You know how it goes, being that you're the king of being a cockhead."

"I'm glad you're finally willing to call me by my proper name"

"Hmm?"

"The King of Cock," Kyle replied. "For so long you've avoided admitting that mine's bigger, and now here we are."

Kris chuckled and rolled his eyes. "We're identical in every single way. Your cock is my cock and my cock is yours."

"You wish. King of Cock," Kyle repeated, adjusting his package for emphasis.

"More like King of Cock-sucking," Kris said, looking awfully proud of himself for coming up with the title.

"You know what the funniest thing about you is?" Kyle asked, leaning forward so he could pack the pipe sitting on the coffee table with weed.

"What is it?"

"Your face."

"You can't say shit like that," Kris laughed. "We share a face. My stupid face is yours."

"Not really, though," Kyle disagreed. "You have a permanently confused expression on yours. Like this..." He contorted his face to reflect how he imagined he would look if he got hit by a two-by-four. "That's what you look like."

Kris sighed and took the bowl from Kyle's hand. "I need this more than you. You don't have to hang out with yourself."

"I actually do," Kyle disagreed. "All day, every day."

"Brutal."

Kyle nodded and grabbed the weed back from his brother. "Tell me about it."

13

For Kyle, being high on Xanax gave him the same feeling he got when he had the most satisfying night's sleep. His weary limbs had a king-size bed to sprawl out on, luxe sheets draped over smooth skin. It was the heaviest duvet that applied the perfect amount of weight on his body, keeping him warm in a room where the thermostat was set to sixty-five degrees—optimal sleeping temperature. It was constantly resting his head on the cool side of the pillow and moonbeams seeping softly between vertical blinds, bathing him in a dreamy haze. All of his nightmares were long since forgotten thanks to a mind as clear as the star-dusted sky.

The standard delivery of cutting and then bumping lines had been replaced by a method that took much more finesse. Kyle's goal was to get the drug to hit him in the head like a freight train rather than putter through his bloodstream like a fuel-depleted golf cart. Initially, while at home, he would find a flat surface to smash up the pills on, but in the interest of efficiency, Kyle found a way to make his drug use portable. Instead of prepping on a flat surface, he rolled up an entire pill inside a twenty-dollar bill. While holding one end, he chewed up and down the seam, rotating and repeating until the pill became powdery before sticking the open end in his nose. One snort gave him instantaneous relaxation. At first, the bitter Xanax drip irritated his throat, but with time he began to crave that drip. He used to only get six hours or so of relief, but his new method had him high all day. He packed his beak as often as possible and lived in a near-constant state of mental leisure.

School was awesome. Kyle sat at his desk listening to the teachers drone on about whatever they were droning on about, and he didn't give a shit if they talked or didn't. He was probably learning via some sort of osmosis because he felt smarter, more capable. He knew the answers to the questions before they were asked. He stayed on point even though he was pretty positive he was pleasantly residing on a different planet, floating in a powdery white galaxy of Xanax. He'd become a strung-out alien, disparate from his flesh and blood classmates. He existed above them in an alternate solar system, one made for people who didn't care to keep their feet tethered to the ground.

Staring out the window while his English teacher explained correct citations for their upcoming research paper, Kyle watched as the cotton ball clouds crawled across the sky. Maybe it would rain, and his feet would be covered with mud as he and Kris crossed the football field to figure out a ride home from school. Though she didn't work, Hope was never there to pick them up. Every day after class, Kyle would mosey out to the parking lot, confident he would find a ride home from a potential customer. Calling his mother was always the last resort considering she would be an hour late and aggravated that she had to leave the house. The thought would have plagued him before, but finding his Xanax high had liberated Kyle, leaving him unbothered by his anxiety, even the pervasive worry that surrounded his mother.

"Kyle," Ms. Johnston called, her tone reflecting what seemed to be an intense level of irritation. The interruption had Kyle begrudgingly headed back down to Earth—at least momentarily. "This is the third time I've had to get your attention. You need to focus on the lesson, or you'll be in big trouble come midterms."

"Sorry," Kyle said, smoothing his hair down as he cleared his throat. Every eye in the classroom was fixed on him, something that would have made him self-conscious weeks ago, but lacked the same effect thanks to his current state of benzo bliss.

She clicked her tongue. "You should be apologizing to yourself. You're the person you'll let down."

"Deep," Kyle mumbled as he nodded his head to show his respect. There were several things he could have said in response, but they would no doubt be more snarky than what Ms. Johnston would appreciate.

"What did you say?" she demanded, walking closer to his chair, hands on her hips.

Though Kyle had often found himself in trouble due to his smart mouth in Texas, he'd flown under the radar for the majority of his time in Tennessee. Evidently, teachers were less likely to kick a kid out of class for putting his head down and not giving a shit than for actually being a distraction. He hadn't minded the time he did in the principal's office at West River, but the idea of having to deal with an administrator he didn't know was entirely unappealing.

"Hmm?" Kyle hummed in an attempt to play dumb. While he didn't consider what he had said to be disrespectful in anyway, he wasn't sure his teacher would agree. The last thing he wanted to do was to obliterate his buzz. It was too good to waste.

"When I told you it was only yourself who you would be letting down, you said something in response. What did you say?"

Ms. Johnston was nothing if not persistent. She reminded Kyle of Matt when he was angling for a fight, but Kyle was lucid enough to know that engaging with his teacher was far more treacherous.

"Um, I don't remember," Kyle lied.

"How about you think about it in detention then?" And with that, she plodded back to her desk to write up the slip.

Kyle idly wondered what had *really* pissed his teacher off. Ms. Johnston was usually understanding and stable, which made it obvious that she was misplacing her frustrations. Maybe she was fighting with her boyfriend, her girlfriend, her boyfriend's girlfriend, her mother, father? It didn't matter anyway. His inaugural detention at Iris Valley High was long overdue. In some *Freaky Friday*–worthy switch up, his brothers had already racked up a handful of infractions each while he maintained a clean record. While Kris and Matt had never exactly been model students, they'd always managed to be less of a thorn in the side of their teachers than Kyle was. Everything had changed when he had tuned out and become determined to go undetected in his classes. Other than the occasional sneaky texting, Kyle hadn't given his teachers a reason to spare him a second glance, so they hadn't.

Ms. Johnston marched over and delivered the citation to his desk as several of his classmates "Ooh"-ed like primary school punks. "You'll all be next," the teacher warned, giving the class further confirmation that she was exceptionally on edge.

For the remainder of the period, Kyle stared at his harried teacher, theorizing about the shitty things that could have happened to her that day and concluding that it was just what life in Iris Valley inevitably did to people. By the time the bell rang, Kyle had completely forgotten what had happened, only remembering that the instructor was upset. He walked in front of Ms. Johnston's desk to grumble a "sorry" before exiting the room. As usual, Emma was waiting outside the classroom door, ready to walk to the cafeteria.

"Hey cutie," she grinned, wrapping her arms around his shoulders and planting a smooch on his cheek. "How's it going?"

"Alright. That savage bitch Johnston gave me a detention," Kyle said, pecking her cheek in return. "I have to text Kris and let him know he's running shit this afternoon."

"Won't you see him in the caf?" she sighed, perpetually irritated by the time he spent on his Blackberry.

"I have to tell Matt too," he replied, bristling at the fact that he had to answer to her yet again. "Brother group text."

Emma nodded. "Got it."

They walked in silence as Kyle messaged his brothers, then some of the frequent flyers who would expect him to be there after school, and finally his dad.

Kyle (12:02pm): Hi Dad.

Dad (12:02pm): Hey Kyle. How's everything?

Kyle (12:02pm): Eh.

Dad (12:02pm): Are you staying out of trouble?

Kyle (12:03pm): Yeah. What about you?

Dad (12:03pm): Mostly. It's too cold to take the jet skis out.

Kyle (12:03pm): Man, I miss the lake.

Though the time spent at the lake house had become different since his parents' divorce, it remained a happy place for Kyle. His family had wasted countless days relaxing on the banks by the water, the warm Texas sun kissing their skin, and while things had gone to shit, the memories couldn't be erased.

Dad (12:03pm): Only a few more weeks until Christmas.

Kyle (12:03pm): Nine is more than a few.

Dad (12:04pm): You're counting.

Kyle (12:04pm): I told you I miss it.

Dad (12:04pm): What about your dad?

Kyle (12:05pm): I miss you, too.

"What are you smiling about?" Emma asked, gently nudging Kyle's arm with her elbow. "You were in a crappy mood two minutes ago. Who's cheering you up?"

Kyle could tell from the look in her eyes that she was jealous, which he found ironic considering she was under the impression he wasn't sexually interested in *anyone*. "My dad."

"I wasn't expecting that," she admitted, with a bashful blush creeping across her cheeks. "You hardly mention him."

Shrugging, Kyle opened the cafeteria door for his girlfriend. "There's not much to talk about. He's not here."

"Do you speak often?"

"Not as much as we should, or as much as I wish we did, I guess."

"Does he know about me?" Emma asked, shyly.

"Um, I think Kris has told him about you. You know, that I have a girlfriend or whatever," Kyle replied, clearing his throat uncomfortably.

"But you haven't?"

"Like I said, we don't talk that often."

"Right," she nodded.

Kyle wasn't an expert in women, but it was apparent that Emma wasn't thrilled with his answers. Perhaps he should've lied and told her that he'd been talking about her nonstop, that his family and friends were getting tired of hearing all the amazing things he said about her. The truth was, aside from the time they spent cuddling in bed watching movies, Kyle barely thought of Emma. It was nice to have the companionship, but she couldn't hold a candle to the drugs, money, or dreams of Texas.

"We're good," he promised, squeezing her hand as they sat down at the crowded lunch table.

Emma was good. Kyle knew that, but when it came down to it, he just couldn't care, which probably wasn't good at all.

14

"Jimmy invited us to Thanksgiving dinner, so be ready to go over there at four," Hope said as she made her way through her morning routine of dishes and aggravating Kyle.

"Absolutely not," Kyle said, astounded that his mother would even mention that he should step foot in Jimmy's house again.

"You're going," she stated flatly without bothering to turn around from her task. "You're lucky he's forgiving and that he found it in his heart to include you for the holiday."

"He's forgiving?" Kyle scoffed. "Please."

"C'mon," Kris sighed, patting the top of Kyle's hand. "Let it go."

"Let it go," Kyle repeated as a surge of seething rage went straight through his skull. "You still don't get it."

"Oh I do," Kris assured, "and that's why I'm telling you to let it go."

It was easy for Kris to tell Kyle to "let it go." He wasn't involved in the altercation that acted as an impetus for Kyle to determine he couldn't trust his mother.

It happened only days after they arrived in Tennessee. As if it hadn't been difficult enough to be ripped from their home, Hope had moved them into Jimmy's house, a short-term arrangement that ended up creating long-term issues. Kyle couldn't deny that he was pissed. Though he would have been angry regardless simply because of the circumstances, it was made even worse by the fact that Hope hadn't worked shit out with their new place prior to the move—her excuse for the accelerated timeline being that she couldn't afford the house in West Lake anymore. Kyle made a concerted effort to avoid his mother and Jimmy. It was nearly impossible for him to look at them, much less converse, so he tried not to do either. Unfortunately, Hope took the avoidance as an inexcusable act of disrespect and made it clear that she wouldn't stand for it.

Growing up, Kyle's dad had been the disciplinarian. When Ken had delivered spankings, Hope comforted the kids, making her husband the enemy for being more physical. Hope had never laid a hand on any of her children, but an after-dinner argument in Jimmy's kitchen changed everything.

"Clear the table, Kyle" Hope ordered as Kyle aimlessly messed with the cooked carrots on the plate in front of him.

Deciding the directive wasn't worthy of a response, Kyle kept his eyes on the orange disks. Push then mush, push then mush, push...

"It's not like you eat anyway," she snarked, shifting to a topic she knew would get a rise out of him.

Instead of feeding into her delusion of his self-induced famine, Kyle ignored his mother in favor of focusing on the carrots.

"Did you hear me?" Hope roared, the sheer volume of her voice demanding Kyle's immediate attention.

"What the fuck?" he exclaimed, surprised by her apparent rage. He stared at his mother for a moment. Her cheeks were flushed an angry shade of crimson and her blue eyes were scary wide.

"Shh," Kris shushed harshly, a hint of panic in his face.

"Don't," Matt warned, shaking his head for emphasis. "Seriously, dude."

"You've really lost your mind," Hope growled, storming to the table and grabbing hold of the nape of Kyle's neck. Her nails dug into his flesh before moving up to grasp a tuft of his hair. Tilting his head back, she crouched over to shove her nose against his. A wave of hot breath inundated his face

as she kept a tight hold on him. "You will never speak to me like that. Do you hear me? You will not speak to me that way."

"Get your hands off of me," Kyle growled, keeping his eyes fixed on his mother's, refusing to back down. While there weren't any comparable incidents to help Kyle predict his mother's next steps, Kyle was still shocked by the fact that she aggressively pushed his head toward the table. "I'm done," he announced, an eerie calm settling over him as he stood up from the chair. "Let's go."

"I'm going to wake Jimmy up," Hope threatened, a warning that would have affected Kyle greatly if he wasn't so done.

There was a split second of doubt when Kyle thought his brothers wouldn't follow and a massive amount of relief when they did. As he sat in the passenger side of Matt's black Volvo 850R Turbo, Kyle hoped his brother was planning to make the long drive to Texas.

"Where are we going?" Kris asked from the backseat.

"West Lake," Kyle decided, irritated by the laughter that followed his statement. "What?"

"We don't have any of our stuff and we're not running away from home like a few imbeciles," Matt said, pushing his key into the ignition. "That's asinine."

"First of all, this shithole isn't home, and second, you're asinine," Kyle retorted, looking down to fasten his seatbelt. When he raised his head a few seconds later, he saw Jimmy angrily charging out of the house, followed by a frazzled Hope. Kyle's heart thumped in his chest, increasingly rapid beats that reverberated through his bones. The last thing he wanted to do was endure another round of berating from his mother and her hick boyfriend.

"Oh man," Kris uttered. "She actually woke him."

"Drive," Kyle demanded, his urgency and insistence growing with each step they took toward the car. "Drive, drive, drive!"

Matt did as he was told, shifting into reverse and flooring the car down the driveway. "Where are we going?" he questioned as he peeled down the street.

"I don't know," Kyle answered, glancing over his shoulder to see if he could get a visual on his mother and Jimmy. Panic set in as soon as he saw

Jimmy's red pickup swinging around the curb. "Shit!" he exclaimed, "Drive faster! They're following us."

"Where am I driving?" Matt repeated, his tone as frantic as his face.

"Um fast," Kris suggested.

"I didn't ask how, *I asked* where,*" Matt huffed.*

"Wherever you can get to fast enough to lose them," Kyle said, wondering what Hope and Jimmy would do to them if they caught up. He had never considered that one day his mother would lose it and actually grab him the way she had. She'd always had more patience—or been more absent—than that. And while he knew Jimmy had a temper, Kyle hadn't experienced it first-hand. It was hard to believe the burly man would ever lay hands on him, but Kyle didn't want to try him.

The country roads around Jimmy's home lacked stop lights, so Matt's effort to lose the truck was effective, at least until they got closer to town.

"Watch it!" Kris cried, as Matt swerved to avoid hitting a bicyclist.

"I saw him," Matt promised. "I got this."

"You're a pretty good driver," Kyle noted, impressed by his brother's prowess. "I didn't know you had it in you."

"I haven't lost him yet," Matt sighed, taking a sharp turn at the intersection.

Jimmy's truck was seconds behind them. Knowing the roads like the back of his hand, Jimmy hit each abrupt direction change with ease.

"Make a quick left before it turns red," Kyle ordered as they sped toward a changing stop light.

"Don't do it," Kris disagreed. "It's been yellow for too long, we'll get fucking t-boned.

As Matt accelerated to the light, it turned from yellow to red. Their bodies jerked forward as the car screeched to a stop.

"Fuck, fuck, fuck," Kyle chanted, sinking further into the seat as if he might disappear. He wished he would. There was no good reason to be involved in a car chase through Iris Valley, Tennessee. His life had changed in the most depressing ways.

Jimmy's cannonball of a fist crashed down on the windshield causing Kyle's stomach to drop to his toes.

"Don't break my window!" Matt yelled, tapping on the gas to scare Jimmy away from the front of the vehicle.

"Unlock it," Jimmy screamed as he ran to the side of the car and attempted to force open the handle. "Now."

A cold sweat began to bead on the back of Kyle's neck as he considered what the fuck Jimmy was planning to do once he got in.

"Green!" Kris called, prompting Matt to speed away.

Kyle peered into the rearview mirror, hoping he'd see the red truck finally giving up. He wasn't so lucky.

Matt shook his in disbelief. "Has she lost her mind?"

"Yes. That's what I've been telling you. That's why we're here. Isn't it obvious now?" Kyle replied, his knee bouncing anxiously as they tore through town.

"Go there," Kris suggested, his finger coming into Kyle's peripheral vision as it pointed toward the police station one traffic light away.

"The police station?" Matt asked, surprised.

"Yeah, there's no way they'll follow us in there."

"Are we just going to go into the parking lot or, like, go in and talk to the cops?"

"We'll go in and talk to the cops," Kyle answered, silently atoning for all the times he had called his twin a dumbass. It was a genius move, one he was sure would rattle Hope enough to give up on her Tennessee dreams and take them back to Texas.

To Kyle's relief, once Matt turned into the lot, Jimmy drove his truck past the station.

It was a victory...until it wasn't.

The first group of officers they told the story to seemed sympathetic to their plight, giving them enough grief for the complaints they'd received from motorists who had witnessed the chase, but balancing it with genuine concern about the situation. While Hope hadn't done anything illegal, it seemed the policemen could recognize how distraught Kyle was. It wasn't until forty-five minutes later when an older sheriff came into the room that it became a problem. After giving Kyle and his brothers a "mind your mother" speech, the cop called Hope and asked her to come down to the station.

"He's always told tall tales," Hope explained with a sigh. "None of what he recounted actually happened."

Glancing from his mother to his brothers and then back again, Kyle tried to understand how Hope could blatantly lie through her teeth to the police and how Kris and Matt could sit there quietly as she did. As he sat flabbergasted in his seat, Kyle considered pressing formal assault charges, and really making his mother pay. His brothers couldn't stay silent under oath. While he was sure his relationship with Hope had forever changed, he wasn't positive he was willing to destroy it completely. So as difficult as it was, Kyle bit his tongue.

"You're coming with me," Hope told Kyle as soon as the four of them exited the front door of the building.

"Coming where?"

"I called my Aunt Sadie and Uncle Jed on the way to the station and they agreed to allow you to live with them until you get your act together," she replied coolly. "In the car now."

"What?" Kyle cried, feeling the air escape his lungs in one long swoosh. "What about Kris and Matt."

"What about them?" Hope grunted, shooing her other boys toward their vehicle. "This isn't about them."

Kyle watched as his brothers got into the car, looking just as shaken up as he did. They were being separated. Kyle was going to live with strangers and his mother was ice in human form.

Though Kyle knew his mother probably wished it would have been horrible, life with Sadie and Jed wasn't bad at all. In fact, he enjoyed the time spent with the older couple. Not only did Sadie and Jed treat him with respect his mother failed to give, they actually liked him and enjoyed having a "young whippersnapper" around to do the chores. It surprised Kyle how often they all laughed together doing inane things like attending street fairs and eating Taco Bell. The constant stream of good reports had Hope knocking on their door after a few weeks, ready to collect Kyle and force him to move back in in time for the first day of classes at Iris Valley High.

"DINNER'S AT FOUR," Hope repeated, refilling Kyle's glass of orange juice. "We're going to have a nice holiday."

"What if I don't want to have a nice holiday?" Kyle challenged.

"You'll have one despite yourself," she replied, matter-of-factly.

And though Kyle was sure he wouldn't, he knew it didn't matter anyway. At least not to Hope.

15

Kyle felt like he was walking in front a firing squad as he entered Jimmy's house. Though he'd only spent three weeks in his mom's boyfriend's place before the car chase debacle, he was inundated with bad memories as soon as he crossed the threshold. He dreaded facing the fat-fingered motherfucker, remembering how his balled hand looked slamming against Matt's windshield. As far as Kyle was concerned, Jimmy was the impetus for everything in Kyle's life going to hell, and he had no interest in breaking bread with him—especially on Thanksgiving. The holiday centered around giving thanks and the last thing Kyle was thankful for was Jimmy.

Kyle was pleasantly surprised to see that Jimmy's living room was full of people. He knew the dinner would be markedly less awkward if it wasn't just his nuclear family and the guy who took his father's place. Distractions were welcome.

"Well, well, well look who showed up," Jimmy greeted jovially as he hugged Matt and Kris. Though his brothers had been a part of the infamous car chase, Jimmy had never held it against them the way Kyle knew he held it against him. It was obvious that Jimmy believed Kyle instigated many of the issues that arose under his roof. It was always easier for dim-witted people to look for a scapegoat rather than to reflect on the psychology behind "unsavory" behaviors.

Watching Jimmy embrace his brothers made Kyle's stomach churn, an inconvenience considering Hope's preoccupation with his food intake. The last thing he wanted was more attention from his mother, though he was aware it was probably exactly what he needed.

"Glad you came, Kyle," Jimmy said through gritted teeth, extending his hand for a shake.

As Kyle reached forward, memories of that big fist hitting the windshield flashed in his mind. While he'd woken up cranky many times, Kyle could safely say that nobody got as perturbed by a rousing as Jimmy did. He wondered what the older man's take on the incident would have been if Hope hadn't frantically gone into his room that day. Maybe he wouldn't have been so overly aggravated and could've talked some sense into Hope. What was done was done, but Kyle hadn't expected that the day would come where he'd be standing in front of Jimmy again, at least not so soon.

"Thanks," Kyle grumbled, feeling his mother's eyes burn into the side of his face. It took everything in his power not to give her a reason to stare.

"I heard that you have a girlfriend," Jimmy began, as if he and Kyle had any business engaging in small talk. "Why didn't she join us?"

"She has a family," Kyle replied. The reason should have been obvious. Maybe Jimmy truly was as obtuse as Kyle had assumed him to be at the start.

"You say that like you don't," Jimmy noted, raising a bushy eyebrow.

"I did not say it like I don't," Kyle disagreed, unsure what Jimmy was angling toward. He was about to tell him not be an instigator when a glare from his mother kept his mouth shut. It wasn't worth it. Neither of them was worth it.

Excusing himself before Jimmy spoke another word, Kyle walked out the sliding glass doors to the backyard. During his short stay at

Jimmy's, Kyle had spent the majority of his time on the deck perched over the woodsy backyard. Though he wouldn't have admitted it then, there was something serene about being among the trees, flat green leaves shading his face from the summer sun, making him feel like he was hidden away, at least for a little while.

To his relief, Kyle's temporary refuge was inhabited by just the person he was hoping to see.

"Hey there, Special K. Long time no see," Mac White said with a big grin stretching over his handsome face. "I thought you were avoiding this place like the plague."

It was funny how 'out of sight, out of mind' had expunged Mac from Kyle's memory bank, despite how much time they had spent together when Kyle had first moved. Though Kyle hated Tennessee from the start, he'd liked Mac. It was difficult to consider him a friend, regardless of the good vibes Mac had given him. Kyle had kept himself closed off from any chance of acclimating, a decision he didn't regret.

Mac was Jimmy's best friend Ray's nephew. He'd moved in with Ray a couple of years prior after a stint in juvie for drugs. Since Ray's house was only two houses away from Jimmy's, they all spent a lot of time together, a fact that had been a sliver of sunshine among the darkness for Kyle. It wasn't that Mac was a cheery person, or even that nice, it was more that he seemed to hate Tennessee, too. He'd been ripped from his life in California and tossed into the hell hole in a similar fashion to how Kyle had been. Unlike Kyle, Mac had made the best of it, or he just numbed himself with enough drugs to try.

"I am," Kyle promised. "I'm avoiding it indefinitely after tonight."

"But tonight you're here," he smiled, holding out a carton of Newports toward Kyle.

"I guess I am," Kyle agreed, nodding a 'thank you' as he took a cigarette and sat down on the wood slat bench next to Mac. "Lighter."

Mac tossed him the Bic, keeping his eyes on Kyle as he lit his cigarette.

"What?" Kyle asked, aware of Mac's attention.

"Nothing," Mac shrugged. "It's kinda like seeing a ghost."

"That's dramatic."

"Not really though," Mac disagreed. "One day you were here, the next you weren't. That's spirit status."

"It's 'cause my mom's a demon."

"She could be worse."

"You hardly know anything about her," Kyle scoffed.

"She's here all the time," Mac reminded. "And I'm here a lot, too."

"Exactly. She's here all the time. She's not with her kids."

Mac shrugged. "You guys are grown. How much raising do you need, you know? She put in her time."

"Hardly."

"So she wasn't around when you were little?"

"You already know this," Kyle stated, recalling how many times he'd talked about Hope's absence to Mac. It was hard to rationalize his frustration while speaking to a guy whose father had left when he was a kid and whose mother was a smack addict. It wasn't lost on Kyle that he didn't have it had it as bad as other people, but their struggles didn't minimize his. It was all about perspective, and in his world, his mother had been an epic letdown.

"Don't you think you should get over it?" Mac asked, the question less accusatory than it could have been with a different inflection. "I mean, how does it benefit you to keep being pissed off?"

"How does it concern you that I am?" Kyle retorted, sick of everyone giving him grief about his feelings regarding his mother.

"It doesn't," Mac said simply. "I hear you have quite the operation built out of your basement. It sounds like you're benefiting from her absence."

"Yeah, we're doing well. I'm surprised you haven't come around to check it out."

"What are you trying to say about me?" Mac laughed. "Should I be offended?"

Kyle grinned and rolled his eyes. It wasn't a secret that Mac was heavy into drugs.

"Honestly, weed's too low-key for me now. I go for a more intense high."

Nodding, Kyle debated whether he should let Mac know he was dealing with the same need. Instead of being honest, he decided to probe to see if they were on the same page with their drug of choice. "What are you doing to get that high?"

"You know," Mac replied breezily.

"I don't," Kyle pressed, "that's why I'm asking."

"The normal stuff: OxyContin, Xanax, Percocet, Morphine and, depending on my mood, Valium or Ativan," he answered, blowing a thick cloud of smoke from his mouth and nose. "My favorite days are the days I can't remember."

"Is that sad?" Kyle wondered aloud.

"Maybe, but I don't have the capacity to feel that either."

"I take Xanax."

"You have a prescription?" Mac asked, his eyes flashing with more life than Kyle had seen throughout their conversation.

"Nope. My mom does."

"So you're self-medicating?"

"Something like that," Kyle confirmed.

"Like a dose a day or...?"

"Like straight up the nose as often as I can," he clarified, much to Mac's approval.

"No shit?"

"You're more excited about this than I am," Kyle chuckled.

"Then you're not doing it right."

"I'm selling it too."

"And just like that I'm interested in your business. My guy gets me Xanax bars for five dollars a pop," Mac stated, seeming to have moved easily into business mode.

"I could hook you up for three a pill," Kyle offered.

"It looks like we're going to be spending some time together again," Mac grinned.

"Cool," Kyle nodded. "I'm in."

"I'm sure you are," Mac laughed. "You're going to get rich off my ass."

"Not for three dollars a pill."

"I was hoping I'd get the friends and family discount and pay two."

"Even less of a chance to get rich off that," Kyle tsked, "so that sure as shit won't happen."

"When did you become such a businessman?"

Kyle wanted to tell Mac he'd always been that way, that business was in his blood, but he figured he was better off being as straightforward and to the point as possible. "When I realized it was my only way out of this place."

"You already got out of Jimmy's."

Kyle grandly waved his hands to present the Tennessee air around them. "*This* place."

"And that's your top priority?"

"That's my only priority," Kyle clarified.

No matter how deep he got into the business or the drugs, Kyle had vowed to leave Tennessee behind and that's what he intended to do. He wouldn't allow himself to get fucked up enough to settle into Satan's asshole. He was better than that.

16

Tennessee wasn't that bad, and it was even more palatable when Kyle was high off his ass on Xanax. The bitter taste dripping down the back of his throat made everything else easily consumed. As often as possible, he reminded himself of how badly he wanted to get away from Iris Valley, but as the days passed—and the powder continued to make its way up his nose—his resolve slowly dissipated.

Kyle had always feared that someday he would become complacent and settle into his crappy life the way so many of his customers had. They should have cared about being stuck in the ass crack of America, but they remained alarmingly unfazed. Perhaps Kyle kept them too high. Maybe he was medicating away his chances of a mass revolt and somehow keeping the teens in Tennessee, even though there were countless better options for every one of them. Perhaps the drugs had already allowed him to become one of them, none of them, nothing of him, and everything he wanted and didn't want to be. He wasn't gay. He wasn't too skinny. He wasn't Hope's son. He wasn't anything. He was gone without leaving, but he should have wanted to go. He shouldn't have had to remind himself of why he wanted to flee; the reasons should have been on the tip of his tongue.

Somehow his mind was as quiet as his mouth, and he'd accepted that he'd become a part of something more than he'd expected to.

Between weed and Xanax sales, he and Kris were raking in an obscene amount of cash, money they wouldn't have had the ability to make in West Lake. The drug trade in the upper-class suburb was saturated with dealers, unlike Iris Valley which now touted Ross Enterprises as its go-to business. Johnny had dropped off the scene completely, leaving them with no competition, big or small. He hated Tennessee, but he loved Xanax. And somehow, just as it had done to Mac before him, the drug had settled him into a place he despised and made it seem alright.

It had happened so fast. One day he was angry and the next the rage flooded from his body, puddles of pissed off feelings lying at his feet, leaving him with nothing left to emote. He was a vacuous shell of an emaciated body, and if he could feel anything, he bet it would have felt a lot like emancipation. His escape had been in front of him the whole time and he had never seen it. There was no reason to get out of Tennessee when all that was left there was his skin and bones. His skeleton made the shithole its home.

"Kyle," Kris whispered. "Kyle."

"Hmm?" Kyle hummed, lifting his head from the cereal bowl he was practically resting it in.

"I've been yelling your name for two minutes," Kris sighed. "You're so fucking out of it, dude."

"You weren't yelling."

"I was yelling," Kris assured.

"He was," Matt confirmed.

"Oh."

"Oh?" Hope questioned, putting down the slice of bacon she was about to bite into. "You're catatonic."

"Nah," Kyle disagreed. "I'm coherent as fuck. I just don't want to talk to any of you."

"Dick," Kris muttered, kicking Kyle's chair as he walked past it to clear his plate. "Maybe you should tell Mom what's going on with you."

"I don't know what you're talking about," Kyle stated, glaring at his twin. It would be just like Kris to blow up the whole operation out of spite.

"Maybe he's talking about your breakup with Emma," Matt offered, shooting a look of warning at Kris. "Do you think that's what he's talking about, Kyle?"

"Probably not," Kyle replied, drawing a groan from his older brother.

"I'm over both of you," Matt announced, getting up to shove his chair under the table.

"You broke up with your girlfriend or she broke up with you?" Hope asked.

"Does it matter?" Kyle scoffed. "A normal question would have been, 'are you okay?' but I guess any level of empathy is unattainable for you."

"Are you okay?" Hope questioned, taking a sip of her orange juice.

"I'm fine."

"I never thought you two made a good couple anyway," she informed him.

"You actually spoke to her, like, twice, so I'm not sure how you came up with that assessment," Kyle stated, turning his attention to his brothers who were whispering to one another beside the kitchen island. "What?"

Four middle fingers answered his question, as Kyle attempted to figure out why the sensitive assholes were so peeved.

"It was easy to see that you two weren't compatible," Hope continued. "She was bigger than you. No girl wants to be bigger than her boyfriend. It makes them feel less feminine."

Kyle stared at his mother, trying to figure out how a person could be so callous and out of touch with everything that was going on right under her nose. Her sons had become drug kingpins and her sole concern was still Kyle's body. He wondered what it was about his weight that affected her so immensely, what it triggered within herself. "I broke up with her."

"You broke up with her?" Hope repeated, surprised. "Wow. Really?"

"Mm-hmm."

"Why?"

"She wanted to have sex all the time," Kyle lied. Since the day Kyle made it clear he wasn't interested in fucking, Emma hadn't pushed, but that hadn't stopped her from attempting to intensify their relationship in other ways. The more she tried to integrate herself into his life, the less he wanted her to be a part of it. The cuddling and companionship wasn't worth the headache she caused him. He didn't need a girlfriend, and he certainly didn't need a wife. It seemed Emma wanted to be both,

"Ex--excuse me?" Hope sputtered, nearly spitting out her food. She dabbed her lips with the napkin like she was proper and Kyle rolled his eyes before bluntly stating:

"She couldn't get enough of my dick."

Matt and Kris laughed while Hope cried, "Kyle!" as if he'd lost his mind.

"I mean, I offered to relieve you of your duties," Kris reminded with a smirk.

"You boys are disgusting," Hope chided, tucking her blonde locks behind her ears. "I didn't raise you this way."

"You didn't raise us at all," Kyle snarked.

"Oh come on," Matt groaned, putting on his backpack. "This again?"

Hope shook her head and rose from the table. "It's never-ending with him."

As she walked out of the kitchen, Kyle called after her, "What, you don't clear your plate? Seems like you didn't raise yourself either."

"Quit it," Kris demanded, kicking the leg of Kyle's chair. "You were better when you were a zombie."

"Hmm," Kyle nodded. "That must mean I'm due for my second dose of the day."

"You've only been up for an hour," Matt said, concern evident in his brown eyes. "Do you think maybe you're doing too much?"

"Obviously I'm not doing enough if I'm getting worked up about dumb shit," Kyle disagreed. "I should've been able to ride that high through Hurricane Hope."

"Why don't you try being sober for a while," Matt suggested. "Remember what it feels like to be present."

Clicking his tongue, Kyle replied, "it feels shitty. It's better this way."

"But are you?" Matt asked.

"It's too early for this."

"And later it will be too late, right?" Kris added. "There's never a good time."

Kyle nodded. "It is what it is for now."

"I think you're spending too much time with Mac White," Matt asserted. "I'm all about getting fucked up, but he's an epic fuck-up, and you are who you hang out with."

"You're just jealous that I'm not a fucking loner like you," Kyle replied, grabbing a can of Mountain Dew from the refrigerator. "That I can hate this place as much as I do and still get popular."

"And that suddenly matters to you?" Kris interjected. "You used to only care about getting out of Tennessee and now you're sabotaging the shit out of our plans."

"Oh yeah? How am I doing that?" Kyle demanded.

"You're putting our potential profit up your nose."

"We're making good money anyway," Kyle tsked. "Stop being so dramatic."

"*I* should stop being dramatic?" Kris laughed sardonically. "That's fucking rich coming from the King of Complaints. You're going to be just like the rest of the losers that end up stuck here."

"Like you ever cared about getting out," Kyle said. "You've been up mom's ass since the divorce—probably before."

"Maybe I do care about getting out," Kris cried, his face flushing pink with anger. "Maybe you never asked how I really felt about it. Maybe I miss my friends back home. Maybe you're not the only person with fucking feelings in this house."

"You should snort more Xanax," Kyle suggested. "It does wonders for getting rid of them."

"So if getting enough money to get out of Iris Valley isn't a priority for you anymore, what is?" Kris questioned, his hands on his hips.

"Nothing," Kyle said plainly, slipping the strap of his backpack over his shoulder. "Literally nothing."

"You'll end up messing it up for all of us," Kris warned.

Kyle shrugged in response, because no matter how hard he tried to—which admittedly wasn't that hard—he just didn't care.

17

While floating aimlessly in a pharmaceutical galaxy, Kyle rarely revisited Earth. It seemed the only person who was able to pull him back down, at least momentarily, was Richard. Perhaps it was because his friend was an alien in his own right. They had never run with the same group, yet they found each other. Maybe it was because they were both different.

Richard (7:45pm): Earth to Kyle.

Kyle (7:45pm): That only works when you're in front of the person waving your hand in their face to get their attention.

Richard (7:46pm): It just worked. You just replied to me, something you haven't done in days.

Kyle (7:46pm): I've been busy.

Richard (7:46pm): Doing what?

Kyle (7:46pm): Nothing much.

Richard (7:47pm): You said you were busy.

Kyle (7:47pm): I lose track of the days so I must be.

Richard (7:47pm): That's alarming.

Kyle (7:47pm): I'm not alarmed, so you shouldn't be.

Richard (7:47pm): What are you doing tonight? You should be able to answer that.

Kyle (7:48pm): I can. I'm going to Mac's place.

Richard (7:48pm): You've been hanging out with him a lot over the last few weeks.

Kyle (7:48pm): True dat.

Richard (7:48pm): True dat?

Kyle (7:48pm): True dat.

Richard (7:49pm): What's he like?

Kyle (7:49pm) Cool.

Richard (7:49pm): Cool in what way?

Kyle (7:49pm): In the way we're not.

Richard (7:49pm): You've always been pretty cool.

Kyle (7:50pm): Eh. I'm okay.

Kyle (7:50pm): His girlfriend's around too much.

Richard (7:50pm): Oh, is it like that?

Kyle (7:50pm): Like what?

Richard (7:50pm): You like him like that.

Kyle (7:50pm): I never said that. Just because I told you I might be into guys, doesn't mean I'm into all of them.

Richard (7:51pm): What's wrong with his girlfriend then?

Kyle (7:51pm): She's a girl.

Richard (7:51pm): So?

Kyle (7:51pm): I don't know. She can be sensitive about things I guess.

Richard (7:52pm): And you don't think guys can be?

Kyle (7:52pm): That's not the point. Would it be better if I said Sarah's too sensitive?

Richard (7:52pm): I think half of the population would appreciate the distinction.

Kyle (7:53pm): Fine. She's too sensitive. With the amount of drugs she does, she shouldn't be like that.

Richard (7:53pm): She does a lot of drugs?

Kyle (7:53pm): Yeah.

Richard (7:53pm): Does Mac?

Kyle (7:53pm): Yeah.

Richard (7:54pm): Do you?

Kyle (7:54pm): I don't know. Not a variety like them.

Richard (7:54pm): But you're doing drugs? I thought you were selling.

Kyle (7:54pm): I'm doing both.

Richard (7:55pm): Just weed though, right?

Kyle (7:55pm): Weed isn't a drug.

Richard (7:55pm): Tell that to the government. So what are you doing?

Kyle (7:56pm): Xanax.

Richard (7:56pm): Do you have a prescription?

Kyle (7:56pm): My mom does.

Richard (7:56pm): And you take it to take the edge off?

Kyle (7:57pm): Something like that.

Richard (7:57pm): That's a relief. I thought you were going to tell me you were into meth or heroin or something.

Kyle decided not to tell Richard that Xanax was known to be just as addictive as the big bad drugs everyone feared. It didn't scare Kyle, though. He knew he could stop whenever he wanted to. He didn't have an addictive personality, and there was no way he would ever let a substance control him.

Kyle (7:58pm): Not even close.

Richard (7:58pm): Good.

Kyle pulled his hoodie up on his head and slid the phone into his back pocket. The November evening was too cold to focus on the messages anymore. With every step he took, Kyle reflected on how unfair and petty his mother was. Kris had been allowed to take his driver's test as soon as he turned sixteen, while Hope had told Kyle he was too immature to drive. It was amazing what years of ass-kissing yielded his twin. Kris wouldn't have to walk the two miles to Mac's if he wanted to chill. He could talk Matt into taking the Volvo. Regardless of how much shit Kyle talked on his mother, he could recognize that she was great at punishing him; first the delay in his license, and then Tennessee. Hope had a penchant for torture.

By the time he knocked on the door of Mac's shed, Kyle could barely feel his hands.

"Hey," Mac greeted as he opened the door and waved Kyle in. "It's cold out there, huh?"

"It's not warm," Kyle agreed, glancing around the shack Mac stayed in. Typically, Sarah would be lounging on the beat-up couch. She wasn't there. "Where's Sarah?"

"Beats me," Mac said, taking a seat. "I'm not her keeper."

"She's usually around," Kyle noted, sitting next to his friend. "Are you worried?"

"Do I seem worried?" Mac grinned, cutting lines of Xanax on the coffee table. "There's worse things to be than missing."

"Like dead?" Kyle laughed. "What the fuck does that even mean?"

"I'm jealous of people who can disappear for a while," Mac continued.

Kyle nodded, wishing he was as high as Mac. He hated to be behind. "Would you want people to look for you?"

"Maybe, but I wouldn't want them to be able to find me."

"It would be cool if they made the effort though. If people gave enough of a shit to start a search party."

"Yup. You have those people. Don't try to pretend that your brothers wouldn't be on the case," Mac stated as he rolled a five-dollar bill and handed it to Kyle.

"They would be," Kyle relented. "But they'd have to be."

"My brothers wouldn't give a shit."

"You have brothers?" Kyle asked, surprised.

"Mm-hmm. You not knowing about them just shows how involved we are in each other's lives."

"And does that bother you? That you aren't in each other's lives?" Kyle questioned, leaning over to bump a line. He relaxed as soon as he felt the burn and sunk back into the cushions as the bitter drip of the drug trickled down his throat.

"No," Mac replied, patting Kyle's knee companionably. "Shit rarely bothers me. I've spent a long time making sure of that."

Kyle couldn't help but notice how similar Mac's answer was to his own responses to the recent questions from inquiring minds. Perhaps mantras of being entirely unbothered were Xanax users' company line. It couldn't hurt business. It was proof that the chemicals worked. The smallest part of Kyle thought of the potential profits while he snorted the product, but mostly the Xanax took care of real-world worries, rendering them completely useless in its glory.

"Damn," Mac grinned, leaning back next to Kyle after his monster hit. "I feel bad for people who don't get fucked up."

"They feel bad for us."

"That's dumb as fuck. Why would they pity people who know how to relax?"

"They probably categorize it differently," Kyle offered.

"Must be tough being dumb."

"We wouldn't know," Kyle grinned.

The shed Mac lived in was rickety as hell and probably a massive fire hazard with his space heaters and janky lighting. The couch, table, and bed barely fit in the small space, but somehow it was awesome. Whenever Kyle was there, he felt like he was miles from everywhere people expected him to be and worlds away from Tennessee. Never had he imagined that he would find solace in a place like that, and he was sure it was the Xanax that made him feel so settled.

In the past, Kyle would have never stepped foot in the space, let alone actively sought it out night after night. There was something to be said for opening oneself to new experiences and a lot more to be said for the draw of the drug. It had turned the shack into a magical place with hazy, thick air and flickering lights. The body on the boy who sat beside him probably didn't hurt either.

There was no way Mac worked out. He devoted way too much of his time to drinking and drugs to make it to the gym, but his abs didn't get the memo that they weren't supposed to be amazing. He had no business being as built as he was, but Kyle wasn't complaining. Not at all.

"Where's Sarah?" Kyle asked, watching the way Mac licked his lips after taking a sip of beer.

"You already asked me that," Mac laughed. "I don't know."

"It's weird that she's not here. She's always here."

"Are you uncomfortable?" Mac asked, tapping the toe of his shoe against Kyle's shin. "Are you afraid to be alone with me?"

Kyle chuckled, the familiar feeling of nervousness drilling through the armor that the mind-altering substances had wrapped him in. "Fag."

"You say it like it's a bad thing," Mac admonished.

"Are you gay?" Kyle croaked, shocked by the admission.

Mac shook his head. "Nope, but I'm not dumb enough to think there's anything wrong with being that way."

"Are you saying I am?"

"That you're what? Dumb enough or gay?"

"Either," Kyle answered, tapping his toe in his sneaker as he awaited Mac's response.

"Maybe, and who knows."

"I'm not."

Mac remained unfazed. "Okay."

"Let's do another one," Kyle suggested, ready to squash the conversation and move onto more lines.

They each took their turn with the Xanax, and by the time he leaned back on the couch, Kyle was completely void of concerns about his sexuality and his previous desire to hide it. When nothing mattered, anything was possible. Placing his palm on Mac's thigh, Kyle looked in his friend's eyes as he moved his hand up toward the crotch of Mac's jeans—a game of chicken. Instead of calling it, Mac doubled down, caging his fingers around Kyle's bulge. Wordlessly, they rubbed their hands over the hardness that bloomed beneath the fabric. As the pressure of their touches increased, Kyle felt compelled to get his mouth on Mac—first on his mouth and then on the hard dick under his hand. Kyle licked his lips, ready to lick Mac's too, and began to lean in, Mac's warm breath releasing in short spurts the closer Kyle came.

The sound of the door opening had them jumping to opposite sides of the couch. With purpose, Kyle cleared his throat and mind of what had almost happened.

"Did you guys start without me?" Sarah chided. "I told you I had a lame-ass dinner with my parents."

"And we were just supposed to sit here and wait for you?" Mac asked, laughing as though the idea was preposterous. "I'm sure you can catch up."

"I hate being sober when everyone's fucked up," Sarah pouted, sitting down on the couch between them. "Cut me two lines," she directed, finally adding a "please," to get Mac moving.

To Kyle's surprise, Mac declared: "Sarah, Kyle wants to pound you. Are you down for that?"

"Oh, hell yeah," Sarah grinned, going along with what Kyle now understood was a joke.

"We should have a three-way and double penetrate you," Mac continued, winking at his girlfriend and then Kyle.

"I could get into some double penetration," Kyle smirked. He was definitely down for sex, as long as Sarah wasn't involved.

They all laughed and Kyle spent the rest of the night high as a kite and enjoying the flight.

18

The sound of his bedroom door opening roused Kyle from the rest he hadn't realized he was taking. Sleepily reaching for the glass of water sitting on his nightstand, he unsuccessfully attempted to remedy the cottonmouth that had been plaguing him for weeks.

"What time is it?" he asked his mother groggily, squinting to read the clock: 7:45pm. "Shit, I'm missing first period."

His room was dark, darker than it should have been at that hour and much colder, too. Though Kyle knew he should have jumped out of bed to get dressed, he didn't. Instead he wrapped his comforter around him and rested his head on his pillow.

"It's nighttime," Hope said, her voice softer and tenderer than he'd heard her in years. "Are you feeling sick?" She pressed her palm against his forehead. Instinctively, he tensed under her touch, holding his breath as if even the air escaping his mouth would make things more awkward. Silently he wished her hand away while simultaneously trying to recall if there had been a time when her comfort felt more comfortable. There was.

Things hadn't always been so strained. Years before she had selfishly disrupted everything he knew, Hope had represented safety to

Kyle—the way mothers were supposed to. He'd trusted her to make decisions that benefited and enriched his life, and for the most part, she had. Hope hadn't been around as much as he'd wished she was, but until she lost her job—and subsequently her direction—Kyle was convinced that the time she'd sacrificed spending with her family had somehow been for the greater good. That all her decisions—no matter how difficult they may have been to swallow—were made with her children in mind. It was evident, especially in moments of timid tenderness from his mother, that Kyle would never be able to trust her intentions. She'd twisted her selfishness into looking like supporting her family was the priority when it had always been about Hope. Maybe if she'd never moved them to Tennessee, Kyle would still believe what he'd wanted to when he was little—that perhaps she was devoted to him like he had felt compelled to be to her. In some deranged way, Kyle knew those feelings remained deep within him regardless of how much he wanted to pretend they didn't. He hated himself for every ounce of love he felt for her. He never thought loving his mother would feel like a weakness, but it did. Kyle didn't want to want her to care for him. He didn't need to need her and be continuously disappointed. He didn't want or need any of it.

"I'm not sick," he bristled, inching away from her hand.

"What is it then?" she asked, leaning over to turn on his bedside lamp.

The sudden flood of light had Kyle squinting and pulling the blanket over his head.

"Nothing," he replied. "Why are you here?"

"Hmm?" she hummed, yanking at the comforter. "Your voice is muffled."

"Why are you here?" Kyle repeated slowly, as if the speed of the sentiment was what had tripped her up before.

"I live here," Hope answered, sans irony. She must have really believed she did.

"You're never here at night," he replied. He didn't have the energy to engage. Maybe he was getting sick.

"Well, tonight I am."

"Why?"

"I'm worried about you," she admitted, pushing a lock of hair off of his forehead. "I know we've had our issues, but you've been even more distant than before."

"More distant than when you kicked me out of the house?" Kyle snarked.

"Don't," Hope warned, shaking her head. "Can we have one conversation without you poking at me?"

"Can we have one conversation where you're actually honest about the things you've done?"

"If we did, we would have to bring up the stuff you did too."

Kyle rolled his eyes. "You're deflecting like you always do."

"And you're projecting."

Groaning, Kyle pulled his pillow over his face, wishing he could suffocate under it. No matter how frustrating life could be, nothing was more insufferable than his mother with her passive aggressive remarks and victim complex.

"I'm worried about you," Hope reiterated as she tugged the pillow away.

"Why?"

"Mothers worry."

Kyle rolled his lips in tight, willing his mouth not to expel the vitriol it wanted to. She was worried about how his behavior may inadvertently have an impact on her. There wasn't a chance she was worried about him the way he used to worry about her. If she were, she wouldn't find it easy to ignore him. He'd be on her mind, the way she used to be on his.

Kyle could remember when he'd first learned about death and the irrational fear that followed the illumination. He was seven years old and entirely unfazed by the revelation that he'd one day die. It wasn't that he never foresaw it happening, it was that it didn't matter that it could happen to him as much as it did that it could happen to his mother. She worked like a dog and it was clear to see that her high profile job took a toll on her. Every night he went to bed praying that his mother would be there when he woke up. More often than not, she wasn't, but a nanny would give Kyle confirmation that she was okay and that settled his mind just fine.

Turning over so his back was to her, Kyle tried to imagine her dying to see if he would feel the same twinge of foreboding fear. He sighed when he did. Did some shared blood really make him so dumb?

"Don't do this," Hope urged, manually turning his shoulder so he was lying on his back.

Kyle stared up at the ceiling.

"Are you on drugs, Kyle?" she asked point-blank, garnering her a glare.

"Are you serious?" he balked, sitting up as soon as she uttered the question. "Where did you come up with that?"

"It doesn't take a genius," Hope replied, shaking her head with disappointment. "I don't know where things went wrong."

"Don't do this right now," Kyle warned. "You don't know anything about my life, what I'm doing, and what I'm not doing."

"Do you think you can get clean on your own or do you need formal rehabilitation?" She paused. "I think you may need rehab, son."

"Are you serious?" Kyle cried. "I sleep through dinner the one night you decide to fucking show and all of a sudden I have a drug problem? What a fucking joke!"

"I'm not laughing," Hope replied. "It's not a joke."

"Yeah, well I'm not laughing either," Kyle grunted, lying down and burying his face in his pillow. "Get out."

"What?"

"Get out," he yelled into the fabric, refusing to lift his head to look at her again. He wanted to forget the faux concern on her face.

"I'm considering sending you to live with your Aunt Kara in Washington D.C. I'm not sure this is the right place for you."

Unable to stop himself from laughing at the asinine statement, Kyle chuckled into the pillow only to quickly devolve into hysterics. "Really?" he asked between hearty laughs. "You're just realizing now that this shithole isn't right for me?"

"I realize that you're not doing well here."

"So, it's not Tennessee; it's me? I'm the problem? Not you or this awful place?"

"You're having problems," Hope clarified. "And I have to figure out a way to help you. Whether it's a change of scenery or a rehabilitation center."

Kyle laughed. "Effective parenting, huh? Figuring out a way to help me? So, you're either going to ship me off or send me to rehab when I'm not even on drugs?"

"You're on drugs," Hope stated bluntly. "You can't tell me that you're not."

"It must be inconvenient for you to be here tonight instead of at Jimmy's, especially since you're here about shit that isn't happening. You're wasting your time."

"It isn't a waste of time when it's about my son's life," she replied. The earnestness on her face was perplexing to Kyle. It was as if she believed her own bullshit.

"My grades are good. I have friends. Everything's fine. Where were you three months ago when things were bad?"

"You were being a brat then. Now I'm actually worried that you have a problem that wasn't just created in your mind."

Kyle rolled his eyes. He never thought he'd fight to stay in Tennessee, but the fact that Hope wanted him gone made him want to stay, "I'm not going anywhere."

"I regret having made it sound like it's a choice."

"So you're kicking me out?" It wouldn't be the first time.

"I'm getting you help," Hope corrected.

"And if I don't go?"

"You will."

"I won't."

"I booked a flight for tomorrow. You're going."

"You wasted your money," Kyle informed her, trying to swallow the swell of emotion that was rising in his throat. He didn't want Hope to see him cry.

"If it's for your health, it couldn't be a waste of money," she disagreed.

"What about if it's for your convenience? Could it be a waste of money then?" He ignored the way his voice was cracking and she did too.

"Pack your things," she directed coolly. "Your flight is at eight."

Watching as his mother exited the room, Kyle vowed that it was the last time he'd see her--but on his own terms.

19

If Mac were still residing in the shed, the decision of where to stay would have been an easy one for Kyle. While the space wasn't big, it was off the grid, which was exactly what Kyle wanted to be. Unfortunately, the late-November temperatures had proven too frigid for Mac's space heaters to handle. Instead of braving the cold, Mac and Sarah were staying in a dive motel that charged nineteen dollars a night for basic, semi-clean, heated rooms. Though they could have probably rented a place for cheaper, Mac was convinced that his credit was an insurmountable issue and putting in the time looking wasn't worth it if it wouldn't pan out in the end. Since it didn't impact him, Kyle hadn't cared enough to argue, a show of apathy that he regretted as he climbed the creaky stairs to Mac and Sarah's third floor hideaway.

"This place is a dump," Kyle stated as Mac pulled the door open for him.

"You're always welcome to not stay here," Mac replied, seemingly unfazed by Kyle's assessment.

Dropping his duffel bag on the worn upholstery of the corner chair, Kyle allowed his eyes to scan the room in its entirety. From the matted carpet to the ripped comforter and recently puttied punch marks adorning the dingy smoke-stained walls, the place was in disrepair.

"How much are they charging you?" Kyle asked, suddenly convinced that the nineteen dollars he had thought was cheap moments before was outrageously overpriced. Maybe he had heard Mac wrong and it was nineteen dollars for a week and not a night.

"Nineteen dollars."

"A week or a night?"

"Have you ever heard of a two-dollar-and-seventy-five-cents-a-day hotel room?" Mac laughed.

"No, but I've never seen one either. And here we are," Kyle replied, hugging his arms over his chest tightly. The idea of actually sleeping in the room was causing him anxiety that the remainder of his Xanax high couldn't taper.

"You could always get your own room somewhere else," Mac snarked.

Mac knew damn well that wasn't an option given Kyle's age. Instead of throwing shit back, Kyle shut up. There was nothing else to say.

"It's really not that bad," Mac continued, softening his affect. Kyle figured he must've looked really pathetic to earn that treatment from his typically brash friend. "Sarah and I have been here for a couple of days and we haven't contracted any weird diseases."

"Well that's hopeful," Kyle muttered, glancing at the single queen bed. "Where am I going to sleep?"

"On the floor?"

Running the toe of his sneaker over a shredded seam of the hunter green carpet, Kyle shook his head. "Not happening."

"The bathtub?" Mac offered, lying back on the bed. The smirk on his face acted as confirmation that he enjoyed torturing Kyle.

"I don't even want to see the condition that thing is in," Kyle uttered, shuddering at the thought. He imagined mildew and a lot of it.

"It's not that bad."

"That's what you said about this room."

"Yeah, well. I'm not a DFW snob."

"Don't blame Dallas for this," Kyle chuckled. "Blame Hope."

"You blame her for everything. May as well pile one more thing on," Mac smirked. "Seriously though, this place is cool. Nobody says shit when we smoke in the room. It's chill as fuck."

"They're probably good with the smoke considering there's no doubt a meth lab down the hall."

Mac's eyes went wide. "No shit? Really?"

"I mean, I don't know. I'm just guessing." Kyle wasn't sure if Mac was aghast by the possibility or completely enamored with it.

"We should get in on that shit," Mac decided. "Do you know how much cash we'd pull in?"

"They blow up all the time and people die."

Mac shrugged. "I love living on the edge."

"How about dying in the boondocks?"

"Either way," Mac said. "Living or dying. What's the difference?"

"Well, one of them means you're alive and the other means you're dead."

Mac nodded. "Yeah I get that. Like I said, either way. So, on the topic of money..."

"I thought we were talking about life and death."

"We need to go back to money. Do you still have a lot of it?"

Kyle narrowed his eyes pointedly. "What are you trying to get at?"

"The rent's not gonna pay itself," Mac stated, taking a swig from the can of Natty Light on the bedside table.

"It's not rent," Kyle laughed, venturing to sit on the very edge of the bed. "I told you I'd pay my part. Business is still booming."

"I guess you get a third of the bed then."

"How does Sarah feel about that?" Kyle questioned, twirling his fingers around tattered strings hanging off the comforter.

Mac clicked his tongue. "I know I'm supposed to care."

"And you don't?" Kyle asked surprised.

"I don't like to hear anyone complain," he answered matter-of-factly. "So there's that."

"That there is. Has she been complaining a lot? About me or

whatever?" Though Kyle was trying to play it off, the idea that Mac chose his comfort over Sarah's was titillating.

Mac and Sarah didn't have a relationship that many would be envious of. It was more a business partnership than anything else. They were in the business of scoring drugs and getting high, and beyond that, there wasn't anything there. Kyle saw the way Mac looked at him, felt the stolen touches, tasted the delicious tension between them. It was a matter of time until Sarah was out and Kyle was in. He couldn't wait, though he wasn't entirely sure what he was waiting for. Mac had no ties to Sarah. Kyle wished he would cut her loose.

"She complains about a lot of things," Mac responded, waving his hand in the air as if he was swatting Sarah's concerns away. "I don't really listen."

"Where is she now?"

"Your guess is as good as mine."

"But she's been here every night?" Kyle asked, hoping the answer was no.

"Two of the three. Hopefully she won't come home tonight."

"Where does she go when she's gone?"

"I don't want anyone answering that question about me," Mac grinned. "So I won't say shit about that."

Kyle nodded, not wanting to know more anyway. He just hoped his new bedmate wouldn't show up.

"Wanna bump some tasty lines?" Mac asked, giving Kyle a flirty smile that screamed of ulterior motives. Kyle wanted him to be suggestive, to be flirty, to be inside of him.

"You know I'm not going to turn that down," Kyle replied, purposely focusing his gaze on the bulge in Mac's jeans. "I'm always game."

"I like that about you," Mac smirked, tossing Kyle a pill bottle. "Crush them up."

"This isn't my stuff," Kyle chided, assessing the label. "Who's Agnes Morrison?"

"Sarah's Mom."

Kyle rolled the vial in his hands. "Should I be worried? Do I have some competition?"

"It's not a competition when your competitors can't compete," Mac stated, nudging his knuckle against the side of his nose. His intention was obvious but Kyle continued to press.

"So it's strictly recreational for her? She's not going to try to flip them for a profit?"

"Look at this businessman," Mac exclaimed, winking at Kyle. "We're not coming for your brand, you beast."

"I just have to make sure I keep everything locked down," Kyle smiled. "Make sure the streets are mine."

"Did you ever imagine you'd be running the streets of Iris Valley, Tennessee? Like, it doesn't seem like it would be something people aspire to do, but it's working well for your pockets.

"No doubt," Kyle agreed as he chewed the edges of his five-dollar bill. Tapping the powder into the pocket, he prepared to suck it all in. A persistent buzzing in his pocket had Kyle passing the hit to Mac and attending his phone.

Richard (8:56am): Where are you?

Richard (8:56am): I'm serious.

Richard (8:56am): I know we don't talk every day, but I'm worried.

Richard (8:57am): Kris texted me and told me you ran away from home.

Richard (8:57am): That you were supposed to be on a plane to D.C.? Some sort of intervention for a drug problem that I didn't know you had?

Richard (8:58am): Seriously, what the fuck's going on?

Kyle (8:59am): Calm down.

Richard (8:59am): It's easy for you to say 'calm down' when you know exactly what's going on.

Kyle (9:00am): Yeah, and I'm saying it, so don't worry that things aren't okay. I wasn't getting on that plane.

Richard (9:00am): I thought you wanted to be anywhere but in Tennessee. What happened?

Kyle (9:01am): My mom wanted me gone.

Richard (9:01am): And...?

Kyle (9:02am): And now I'd rather rot here than leave.

Richard (9:02am): That's mature.

Kyle (9:02am): That's sarcasm.

Richard (9:03am): Good catch.

Kyle (9:03am): You don't understand.

Richard (9:03am): Explain it to me.

Kyle (9:03am): I will one day. Not today.

Richard (9:03am): Are you too busy getting high?

Kyle stared at his phone screen, debating whether it was worth responding to such a blatant accusation. It wasn't as though he tried to hide what had been going on, but he didn't need his friend throwing it in his face. It felt like a betrayal, and the last thing Kyle needed was to be fucked over by another person he cared about. It was further confirmation that emotions were a liability and Xanax kept him as safe as it kept him numb.

Tossing his phone to the far side of the bed, Kyle smiled at Mac who was handing over the freshly packed pocket. He couldn't wait to not worry about anything but the next line. Lying next to Mac on the ratty bed, Kyle let the drugs clear his mind and his friend nonchalantly study his body. Somehow, he felt bigger under Mac's gaze. The Xanax mitigated his desire for muscle mass and made him feel like he was worth looking at. Especially when the eyes drinking him in were Mac's.

20

Hours turned into days with the motel room's blackout shades being surprisingly effective at fucking up Kyle's internal clock. From lying in bed wedged between Mac's warm body and the wall to sitting in the chair watching figures move rhythmically under the sheets, his life had become a cycle of staring, snorting, and wondering why he was still in Tennessee. The chance to live with his aunt in Washington D.C. would have been a blessing weeks ago, but Hope unilaterally making the determination that he had to go had kept him in the place he wanted to be the least. He admonished his hurt for turning into a futile anger that forced him to function in a way that spited himself. He should have gotten on the plane and made his mother believe that she had won. Kris was right. Kyle consistently punished himself in hopes of getting back at Hope, and it never worked. Selfish people weren't impacted by the suffering of others. It was the nature of the beast, and his mother was a monster. He needed to stop screwing up his life to stick it to his mother or he would be stuck in shitty situations and she would remain unfazed.

"Your phone's out of control," Sarah grumbled, sitting up in bed to throw the device at Kyle as he feigned an attempt to catch it.

"Sorry, it must've fallen out of my pocket," he muttered, squinting as the bright light of the screen flooded his eyes.

"You haven't worn pants in four days," Mac laughed, wrapping his arms around Sarah's waist.

Kyle gnawed on the inside of his cheek. Mac would know, he had his hands on Kyle whenever Sarah turned her back. Try as he might, Kyle couldn't figure out what Mac's deal was. It was obvious his friend was attracted to him, but he never really made a move aside from rubbing his cock and sneaking kisses on his neck. Kyle was perpetually worked up and there was no denying that he wanted more from Mac. The older boy was hot and charismatic in all the ways Kyle wished he was. The more time they spent together, the more Kyle was drawn to Mac, yet regardless of how reciprocal Kyle believed the attraction was, Mac never got rid of Sarah. While his feelings for Mac had grown, Kyle's respect for Sarah had plummeted. It wasn't as though he was so keen on her to begin with, but as the days passed, he found it increasingly difficult to put up with her at all. Mac wasn't exaggerating when he said she complained a lot. Kyle couldn't figure out how a person so fucked up on drugs could find so many things to be pissed off about. It was terrifying to consider what she would be like sans inebriation. Mac could do better. He could do Kyle.

"Yeah, well, you seem okay with it," Kyle stated, licking his lips as Mac hid a grin.

The anger in Sarah's glare nearly seared Kyle's skin off. "What's that supposed to mean?" she demanded, shrugging Mac off of her. She turned to her boyfriend. "What does he mean by that?"

"He's just fucking around," Mac said easily, tracing his fingertips over the curve of her cheekbone.

"I told you I don't like it," Sarah whispered, as if Kyle wasn't five feet away from her in a quiet room.

"Shh," Mac hushed, running his typical game. Leaning in, he slotted his mouth against hers, prompting Kyle to look anywhere but at the kissing couple, even if it meant checking his phone which had been inundated with messages from his family for the past several days.

Kris (6:23am): Where are you?

Kris (6:41am): You better show up to school today.

Kris (7:12am): I'm serious. This is the last day before they get you for truancy.

Kris (7:48am): You'll get tossed in juvie.

Kris (8:04am): Your puny ass won't last a day in juvie. You're so fucked.

Kyle (8:12am): Is mom going to get fined?

Kris (8:13am): Is that really what you're concerned about?

Kyle (8:13am): Yup.

Kris (8:13am): Of course she'll get fined.

Kyle (8:14am): Good. You need to hide the citations.

Kris (8:14am): What?

Kyle (8:14am): Hide them so she can't pay them and they'll throw her in jail.

Kris (8:15am): You're demented. Where are you?

Kyle (8:15am): Don't worry about it.

Kris (8:16am): Oh yeah, because that's totally possible. I'm not fucking around anymore. Tell me where you are.

Kyle (8:16am): Why? So you can tell Mom?

Kris (8:17am): You're an idiot. Have you ever stopped to think that maybe you're wrong? You're obviously strung out on drugs and instead of giving you any shit for it, Mom offers you a way out of this place which is all you've wanted for months.

Kyle (8:19am): She wasn't offering me a way out. She was kicking me out. There's a big difference.

Kris (8:20am): Kicking you out to a place you've wanted to live for as long as I can remember. This should have a no-brainer for you, but you have no fucking brain. You should've just gone with it.

Kyle (8:23am): That's easy for you to say.

Kris (8:23am): It's easy for anyone to say. You're the only person who makes anything difficult.

Kyle (8:24am): Hardly. Remember why we're here to begin with.

Kris (8:24am): You typed "here." So you're still in Tennessee then?

Kris (8:24am): It's just like you to run away and then NOT leave the place you've been bitching about for months.

Kyle (8:25am): What are you trying to say?

Kris (8:26am): I'm effectively saying that you're a pussy.

Kyle (8:26am): You're my twin. That makes you a pussy, too.

Kris (8:26am): We're nothing alike. Get your butt to school before you get in more trouble than you know how to handle, and then take over the afternoon shift. I'm tired and deserve a day off.

Kyle (8:28am): When did drug dealing get so exhausting?

Kris (8:28am): When my useless business partner decided to fuck off and leave me with ALL OF THE WORK.

Kyle (8:29am): I'm not going to her house.

Kris (8:29am): I know this is going to be hard for you to understand, but she's still not around. It's not just you she avoids, it's all of us.

Kyle (8:30am): Whatever. I'm not going there.

Kris (8:31am): Then I'm spending your cut for this month. I'm not gonna give you money when you're not doing anything.

Kyle (8:32am): I got the whole thing off the ground. You'll be paying me in perpetuity for that.

Kris (8:32am): Where should I send your check?

Kyle (8:33am): Check lol. Wouldn't you like to know? I'll come for my cash soon.

Kris (8:33am): I'm not giving you anything. I've been busting my ass and you've been gone.

Kyle (8:34am): Bring it to school today.

Kris (8:34am): I'm already at school. You're an hour late. You have another two until you're marked unexcused...and then truant.

Kyle (8:35am): I'll be there. Go home and get my money at lunch.

Kris (8:35am): Fuck you. You weren't even asking about it until I brought it up.

Kyle (8:36am): Until you brought it up and told me you weren't giving it to me. Now I want it more.

Kris (8:36am): I'll see you after school then. Come around and I'll give you your cut and then you can take care of the afternoon bunch.

Kyle (8:37am): I told you I wasn't going to her house.

Kris (8:37am): You're impossible.

Kyle sighed and stood up shakily from the chair. He couldn't remember the last time he ate a meal, and as he pulled on his jeans, the loose legs told him it had been a while.

"Where are you going, String Bean?" Mac asked, turning on the lamp.

Kyle knew his friend had flicked the light on to get a better view of his body, so he gave Mac a little show, taking a few extra moments to rifle through his duffel bag until he chose a sweater.

"He's so skinny," Sarah tsked, making it clear she didn't enjoy the view. The disgust in her voice had Kyle regretting not hiding his chest from her judgmental eyes.

It was sad how fast Kyle could go from feeling confident to completely deflated based solely on the tone of a random druggie's assessment of his build.

"He can't help that he's thin. Some guys are built small," Mac said. And just like that, any touches or compliments he'd given Kyle melted away.

"He could eat a fucking hamburger," Sarah asserted. She turned her face toward Kyle as if he hadn't heard the entire conversation. "I can see every vertebrae of your spine when you lean over. That can't be healthy."

"Why are you worried about it?" Kyle asked. "You're that concerned about my well-being?"

Sarah was rendered silent, but Mac chimed in with a cheeky grin. "I am. We have rent due for next week."

Kyle thought about correcting him, about telling him that it wasn't rent for the fortieth time, but he decided against it. He had things to do.

"Where are you off to?" Mac asked as he lit a cigarette for Sarah and then one for himself.

"It's not like you to leave the room."

"I have to get some cash from my house."

Both Mac and Sarah appeared to be immediately invested in the statement. "Oh yeah?"

"Yeah," Kyle replied. "Kris told me he wasn't going to give me my cut for the month, so I'm going to make sure I get paid."

"You know where he keeps it?" Mac questioned, tapping his fingers on his kneecap. "You should take it all."

"Nah. I'm good with just my cut."

"It must be a lot," Sarah uttered.

"It's enough," Kyle answered, zipping his coat.

"Enough that he'll actually step foot in Hope's house to get it," Mac added with a laugh. "It sounds like we're going to have a big steak dinner tonight. Put some meat on those bones."

"I'm down," Kyle grinned.

Steak sounded good. So did bones.

21

Kyle woke up with a belly full of steak and a surprising amount of space around him in the bed. Stretching his arms over his head, he relished in the feeling of being satisfied. It had been so long since he had a good meal, and though it wasn't home-cooked, it hit all the right spots. Though it wasn't out of the ordinary for Sarah to be gone when Kyle woke up, it was unusual for Mac to leave the room during the day. It had to be daytime. Kyle checked the time on his phone to confirm: 10:26am. Weird.

Rolling out of bed, Kyle flicked on the light switch, shocked to find his belongings strewn across the floor.

"What the fuck?" he grumbled, walking closer to his things. Immediately, he dropped to his knees and began tossing the articles aside to search for the envelope of money he had buried at the bottom of his bag. "No," he sighed, shaking his head vehemently as if the action would reverse time. "No, no, no. Oh shit." Rubbing his palm over his forehead, Kyle tried to catch his breath. They wouldn't. Even if Sarah would, Mac wouldn't. There had to be an explanation. He hurried to the closet where they kept their stuff and gasped when he saw it was completely empty. "Fuck," he cried, chucking a hanger across the room. As if his luck couldn't get worse, Kyle watched in slow motion as the hanger hit the base of the ceramic lamp and sent it crashing to the floor. His aim had never been so good, and his life had never been such a mess. He laughed sardonically as he stood in the middle of the room, surrounded by the wreckage of his poor decisions.

He should have known better than to trust a couple of addicts. Addicts couldn't be trusted, and now Kyle knew that he couldn't be trusted either. He used to have faith in his decision-making abilities. Kyle-before-Xanax would have never let himself get taken advantage of the way Kyle-after-Xanax had. He should have seen the red flags, but he was too busy playing grab-ass with a guy who never actually wanted him to open his goddamn eyes. Pressing the heels of his hands against those very same eyes, Kyle hoped that he'd lift his lids and see the lamp magically pieced back together, Mac and Sarah asleep in the bed, and all his clothes folded neatly in his bag. Unsurprisingly, when he opened up, he found that everything was still a mess, and he was still an idiot.

Crawling across the bed to get to his phone, Kyle dialed Mac's number and punched the pillow when his former friend didn't answer. As a foreboding swell of anxiety bloomed from his chest, Kyle scrambled to the dresser to grab his pill bottle. He needed to take the edge off.

Empty.

Fighting to get his breath under control, he opened every drawer, hoping he'd misplaced the drugs he knew Mac had stolen. What a fucking animal! As if it wasn't bad enough that they robbed him blind, Mac and Sarah didn't even have the decency to leave anything behind for him to medicinally cope with their betrayal. It was too much. Throwing himself down onto the nasty floor, Kyle started to cry, softly at first until he realized that each tear did its job to abate the awful pressure in his chest. Then came the loud cleansing wails. He couldn't remember the last time he'd cried with such intensity, though over the past several years there had been plenty of reasons he could have.

Kyle had never been as alone as he felt, even in Tennessee. Before he'd isolated himself from his brothers, they'd been there—at least in body, and there was something soothing about proximity. Though their presence never made the move okay, their absence reverberated as he cried alone in the disgusting hotel room. It was his fault he was by himself, and he vowed to remember that when Kris and Matt inevitably shunned him for losing a crazy amount of money.

Letting five hundred dollars sit unlocked in a drug den was so stupid that Kyle figured he deserved what he got, but it didn't make the pill any easier to swallow. Not only did the act embarrass him, but it was mortifying to think that Mac and Sarah planned the whole thing behind his back. He had been smitten enough to believe that he and Mac had something special, that his friend was just biding his time with his bitchy girlfriend—but clearly it was him who Mac was tolerating. Mac had kept Kyle around as long as he needed to benefit from him, and as soon as he did, he was gone.

"I don't want to buy that lamp," Kyle mumbled, rubbing his forehead. It was the least of his problems, but the broken shards of glass were a not-so-subtle reminder that everything had become a mess that he couldn't afford to properly clean up.

Forcing his body off the bed, Kyle wiped his damp face with a discarded t-shirt before shoving it into his bag along with all the rest of his wrinkled clothing. Despite his best efforts to steady them, his hands trembled as he retrieved the rest of his belongings. Silently, he prayed that the money would magically appear, that it was all an awful mistake, a horrible misunderstanding. He knew better than to get wrapped up in idealism. He'd done that for long enough.

Kyle buttoned his coat and tied his scarf loosely around his neck. He knew where he needed to go and that he would soon be admitting defeat to the people who were waiting for him to walk through the door with his tail between his legs. He didn't necessarily think Kris and Matt would find joy in his failures, but he knew they would be glad he needed them, even in the most basic sense. Kyle spent a fair amount of time trying to convince them, and himself, that he was independent, a mission that felt like a farce after he got taken by scammers he thought were friends.

The freezing air nipped at his ear lobes as Kyle power walked past the building where the front desk and registration were housed. The last thing he needed was to draw Sidney's attention. Not only was the old dude a big talker, he was the money man at the motel, always ready to collect. Kyle had never found Sidney's post to be an intimidating one, a luxury the he could attribute to the padding in his pocket. His sudden lack of cash made the possibility of running into Sidney a much more stressful experience than Kyle had expected. Picking up his pace, he practically jogged past the door. It wasn't until he was half a mile down the road that he allowed himself to let out a full exhale. He didn't know why he had held it in, but his lungs were burning and his head was heavy. Perhaps he was in the middle of a panic attack or experiencing withdrawals. Either way, he wasn't doing well, and there was nobody to blame but himself—and maybe Hope. At least a sliver of his misery was always hers, and maybe hers was his too. They were bonded by blood and bound by expectation, and the fact that they struggled to get along made everything exponentially worse. Regardless of how awful it was going to be to explain things to his brothers, Kyle knew it wouldn't compare to having to face Hope. He should've gone to D.C., should've taken the opportunity to carve out a new life for himself away from Tennessee, Texas, and everything he'd known. At least then his floundering would have made sense. Kyle would've had time to "find himself" in a way that would have prevented him from getting so damn lost.

The long walk to Hope's house was short thanks to the dread consuming him. It was unfair that places he didn't want to go felt nearby, while everywhere else was light-years away. Opening the door to the basement apartment, Kyle's anxiety grew exponentially. His first priority needed to be Xanax, just as it had been for the past couple of months. He took the steps by twos, hurrying though he knew nobody was home. He had a few hours before his brothers showed up and he needed to be high to cope with the amount of shit they were going to throw his way.

As soon as Kyle saw the vial, he was overcome with relief. Momentarily, he wondered if the drug had as much of an effect on him as the idea of the drug did. Was it a powerful placebo that had convinced him he needed it to get by? A quick crush and snort ushered in an overwhelming sense of calm and assured Kyle that Xanax was, in fact, the real thing and that he definitely needed it to get by.

He floated back down to the basement on a protective cloud of care, safe and sound with nobody around. He had nothing to fear and less to lose, and everything was okay. Kris and Matt would come home after school, and he would be there. He didn't need to explain himself; he just needed to chill and wait for it all to pass the way it always did. Settling into the couch that was much cleaner than he remembered, Kyle turned on the television and watched people talk about problems that weren't his. There was solace in the distance. He didn't fear the feeling of being far away from everything the way he had an hour before. His empty wallet was as unsettling as the empty house, but his mind was the most empty of all. Nothing mattered, and everything was okay—just the way he'd hoped it would be, the way it had to be. Time would pass, his brothers would come home, and Kyle would be there. It would be like any other day. What had he been so worried about anyway?

22

"Look who decided to show his face," Kris exclaimed as soon as he opened the basement door.

"I'm pretty sure my face isn't showing," Kyle grumbled from where he was lying face down on the couch. It was so comfortable. He didn't recall it being so comfortable. It almost made the journey back to the house worth it.

A hard smack on the ass prompted Kyle to turn over and look his twin in the eyes. "What?"

"You don't think it's weird that you show up and take a nap on the couch like you haven't been missing in action for weeks?"

Kyle shook his head as he pulled up the hood of his sweatshirt. "Not really."

"Well I do," Kris stated, sitting on the arm of the couch and staring down at Kyle. "Where have you been?"

"You don't want to know."

"I do," Kris disagreed. "That's why I asked."

"It's not worth discussing."

"It kind of is. You were gone for a while and you don't look good."

"Always with the insults," Kyle chided, tugging the drawstrings so the hoodie was tighter around his face.

Leaning over, Kris lifted the hem of Kyle's sweatshirt to expose his slimmer-than-usual stomach.

"Stop it," Kyle complained, immediately yanking it back down.

"Did you eat anything over the last few weeks? You're emaciated," Kris admonished. "Like, way too skinny."

"Is it news to you that we're skinny? We were born this way and nothing's changed."

"Don't lump me in with you. I'm thin, but you look sick, like knocking-on-death's-door skeletal."

"Please," Kyle scoffed, rolling his eyes at Kris' assessment. It was the lowest common denominator, and the one that his family consistently sunk to. It was as if they exploited his visible weakness as a means to make themselves feel bigger, appear stronger. "I'm hardly skeletal."

"Whatever you have to tell yourself," Kris sighed. "Seriously though, where have you been?"

Kyle debated telling Kris exactly what had happened during his brief stint as a runaway, a train of thought that was unexpectedly mortifying. His twin had been privy to most of the embarrassing stories he had to share throughout his life, so it was odd for Kris to be on the outside of something that would no doubt impact Kyle for a while. It took more gall than Kyle thought it would to come clean.

"I was staying at the motel on I-93 with Mac and his girlfriend," Kyle confessed, hating the way Kris' eyes went wide at the admission.

"What happened to his shed?"

"I guess it's too cold in the winter, so they got a room at that motel and I crashed with them."

"You're not a 'crasher,'" Kris stated, shaking his head. "You don't just 'crash.' You're the kid who Dad had to pick up from sleepovers in the middle of the night because the accommodations weren't comfortable enough for your bougie ass. What business do you have staying in a shithole with a couple of meth-heads?"

"They weren't doing meth," Kyle muttered, as if it made a difference. "And it wasn't that bad." The lie burned as it rolled off his tongue. Even before it got truly awful it was horrible. It was so terrible that he wanted to forget any of it had ever happened, but the betrayal ensured that he never could.

"What a relief," Kris deadpanned. "What were they doing then?"

"Just pills. Same as me."

"And how's that working out for you?"

"How's what working out for me? The pills?" Kyle asked, smoothing his eyebrows with his fingertip. The conversation wasn't going in a good direction. He could tell from the glint in Kris' eyes that his brother was preparing to go in hard.

"Yeah. Being an addict. How's that working out for you?" Kris pressed, pursing his lips. If he was trying to hide his aggravation it wasn't working.

"I'm not an addict."

"Says every addict ever."

"I'm not," Kyle repeated, wondering if perhaps he was.

"Do you know who ends up *crashing* in dive motels with their burnout friends?"

"People who are down on their luck and have a bitch for a mother," Kyle offered.

"We have the same mom. When are you going to stop acting like a victim?"

"Who's acting like a victim?" Matt asked, as he walked into the basement. When he caught sight of Kyle, he nodded his agreement. "Wow, yeah. I mean, I knew you were talking about him, but I didn't think he'd be here."

"He has a name," Kyle said, sitting up as Matt nudged him to make room on the couch.

Matt shrugged. "I forgot it because you've been gone so long. No texts, no calls ..."

"Tell Matt where you've been staying."

Kyle glared at Kris, who clicked his tongue in response.

"I'm not even staying there anymore," Kyle grumbled, wishing he would have come up with a more respectable destination or, at the very least, made one up for when the time came to share where he'd been with his brothers.

"That's news," Kris noted.

"Not staying where?" Matt asked.

"He was at the motel on I-93 with Mac and his trashy girlfriend," Kris informed.

"The dilapidated building two miles away?" Matt questioned, pausing as he packed the bowl on the coffee table. "Are you serious?"

Kris nodded as Kyle stared at the wall in front of him.

"That place is like a brick and mortar staph infection," Matt cringed. "I hope you Cloroxed the hell out of every surface."

"It wasn't the first thing on my mind," Kyle stated, refusing to spare a glance in either of his brothers' directions.

"Addict," Kris asserted. "Addicts don't Clorox."

"Is that an actual thing?" Matt chuckled, passing the bowl to Kyle.

Instead of taking a hit the way he typically would, Kyle waved it away. "Maybe you two are addicts too. You smoke your weight in weed."

"Nah, we smoke yours," Matt corrected, "so like two ounces." He turned to Kris. "He's skinnier, right?"

Kris nodded the affirmative as Kyle sighed and reminded them, "I'm right here."

"What kind of brothers would we be if we didn't call you out on your shit?" Matt said, trying to pass the pipe again.

Though Kyle was aware that he was once again punishing himself on principle, he didn't care. He didn't need their drugs, their disrespect, or their attention. He didn't need anything from them.

"Less annoying ones," Kyle replied. "It's something to aspire toward."

"Mm-hmm," Kris hummed, unimpressed. "So, why aren't you with your buddies in the flophouse?"

"It wasn't a flophouse, and they weren't my buddies," Kyle said, though the motel probably was a flophouse, and he'd definitely considered Mac a friend. The truth would have made the happenings even more depressing than they already were, which seemed like an impossibility. If the bullshit of the last several days had taught Kyle anything, it was that things could always get worse.

"They weren't your buddies," Kris laughed sardonically. "Alright, Kyle. Why'd you stay with them then?"

"Because it was a place to go."

"Why aren't you there now?" Matt asked as a plume of smoke escaped his lips. "I'm happy you're here, but I'm wondering why you're not there."

Kyle steeled himself as best as he could before admitting: "they fucked me over."

"How did they do that?" Kris questioned, appearing to be equal parts concerned and pleased.

Though it pissed him off, Kyle understood Kris' position. He couldn't imagine what it would be like if one day Kris disappeared, leaving him behind without any evidence of a fleeting thought. Even the notion of that abandonment cut deep. He hadn't considered that his absence could hurt Kris. He wondered if his twin would've taken into account how it would have affected him and hated the way his mind betrayed him and told him that there was no doubt that Kris would have. It made Kyle think about what was wrong with him that he was so inconsistent. Had he been better before the Xanax? Or had he just believed he was?

"They stole some of my money," Kyle answered, doing his best to play off the statement as if it wasn't a major deal, even though he was well aware it was.

"They did what?" Matt sputtered, coughing out his hit. "How much money?"

"What money?" Kris demanded, giving Kyle a look they saved for their angriest moments.

"What money, Kyle?"

"My half of this month's earnings."

"Your what?" Kris cried. "You haven't done anything. You didn't get a cut. That was my money!"

"You don't decide what cut I get. We went into this thing together and that's how it is," Kyle stated matter-of-factly. "I took some time off, but it's still my operation."

Kris jumped up from his perch to pace the length of the basement. "You can't be serious."

"I'm dead serious," Kyle promised, posturing more than he should have been with absolutely nothing to back his attitude.

"How much did they take?" Kris demanded, in the midst of an epic display of disappointment. The whole scene would have been comical if Kyle had been in the mood to do anything other than hate himself.

"My cut," Kyle reiterated, garnering a series of swears from Kris.

"Your cut is nothing. You didn't earn shit. So how much of my money did they take?" his twin inquired.

"This isn't going to end well," Matt decided, standing up from the couch. "I'm going to ..." he paused as if he was searching for an excuse to get out of the basement, "get the fuck out of here."

It wasn't a bad idea. Kyle wanted to leave too, but he didn't have the luxury.

"It was my five hundred bucks," Kyle said. "That's what they took."

"You did twenty dollars' worth of work, if that!" Kris cried. "You have a ton of fucking nerve, you know that?"

"I don't know anything anymore."

"Your self-abasing attitude isn't going to throw me off your scent," Kris promised. "You can mess up your life as much as you want to, but don't touch mine. That's when I'll lose my goddamn mind, when you come for my shit. I'm not going down with you."

"I'm not going down at all," Kyle bristled, standing up and brushing off his pants as if he had a modicum of dignity left. Everything was a travesty and he couldn't remember the last time he'd washed the jeans he was interested in appearing to be worried about. "I'm good. You'll see how good I am soon."

He walked into his bedroom surrounded by a bubble of confidence, which promptly popped as soon as he locked the door behind him. Kyle had gotten in over his head and was paying the price. He couldn't admit defeat, so he cried into his pillow instead. And when it was saturated with his tears, he turned it over and wept some more.

23

It shouldn't have bothered Kyle that it took Hope three days to notice that he was home, but it did. She wasn't tuned in to begin with, so it wasn't surprising that she'd altered her breakfast-every-morning schedule to a bare minimum biweekly drop-by. It seemed the small sacrifice of spending less than an hour a day with her kids had been too difficult for Hope to maintain. Honestly, Kyle was shocked she'd kept it going as long as she had. He thought she would have found a way to phase out the obligation months sooner. After all, she'd honed her ability to avoid her kids for years. Either way, it was good to get back into the swing of things without Hope breathing down his neck. Though Kris and Matt claimed they didn't tell their mother that Kyle was home, Kyle still wondered if they had and if Hope just didn't care enough to check in on him.

It wasn't until the house came crashing down that Kyle saw his mother's face again. It had started as an ordinary Saturday morning for Kyle and his brothers. They sat on the basement couch eating Lucky Charms, playing video games, smoking weed and bickering—their favorite pastimes.

"You're ripe, dude," Kyle complained, crinkling his nose as Matt stretched his arms over his head in the midst of an overdramatic yawn. "You need to scrub your nasty ass pits."

"You need to gain ten pounds," Matt retorted.

"Those two things are, like, not equal at all in the amount of effort it takes to achieve them," Kyle replied, tossing a stale marshmallow at Matt's mouth. It unceremoniously rolled off his chin and down his chest.

"Don't waste the marshmallows," Kris chided, plucking the rainbow off Matt and popping it into his mouth. "Those little fuckers are gold."

"He's dirty!" Kyle cried. "His shirt has sweat stains all over it. Spit that out!"

"Says the guy who stayed in a roach motel for weeks," Matt tsked. "You're perpetually grosser than me now. Like, you have me beat forever."

"You're pretty much a walking disease," Kris agreed, earning a middle finger from Kyle. "A disease that can't afford to be medically treated because it got all its money stolen."

"The good thing about having a business where you're making a ton of money is there is always more money to be made," Kyle said, nonplussed by the hell Kris had been serving him since he came clean about what happened in the dirty hotel room.

"The only reason the business survived your breakdown is because *I* kept it alive," Kris reminded. "So think about that when you talk about the business *you* have."

"I helped," Matt asserted.

"That's not my point," Kris said. "The point is that Kyle didn't."

"Yeah, I got that, but you can't just sit here and take full credit for shit I did too."

"You know what?" Kris began, tapping the side of the pipe. "You do smell."

"You two are pricks," Matt huffed, taking one last bite of his cereal before placing the bowl on the coffee table and heading up the stairs.

"Really?" Kyle called after him. "You're going upstairs, and you can't even take your dish?"

Matt responded by slamming the basement door and hippo-stomping up the next flight of stairs.

"Ugh, the cereal's going to dry out and stick to the bowl, you dick," Kris mumbled, shaking his head. "You'd think a wake-and-bake session would chill him out."

"He's needs a Xanax. Weed doesn't chill you out like a Xanny can."

"Nobody's taking advice from you," Kris said as if it was ludicrous for Kyle to interject the statement at all. "Literally nobody."

"Nobody?"

"Not one person," Kris confirmed.

"Good to know," Kyle nodded, laughing when Kris tickled his ribs. "Stop."

"You're not even going to fight it?" Kris chuckled. "You're just going to accept the berating without getting mouthy?"

"Another point for Xanax," Kyle replied, elbowing his twin away. "Honestly, it's the best."

"I'm not going to sit here and listen to you wax poetic about your drug addiction."

"Not addiction," Kyle corrected. "Drug appreciation. There's a difference."

"Yeah, I don't know about that," Kris tsked, lighting the pipe and taking a hit.

"What about your addiction to weed?"

Kris laughed. "People don't get addicted to weed."

"They can."

"They don't, but people get super addicted to Xanax."

"Is 'super addicted' the highest level of addiction?" Kyle mused. "I mean, you're suddenly an addiction specialist, right? Is that in medical books and stuff?"

"I'm spouting off facts and you're getting annoyed because they're inconvenient," Kris noted. "Which has to be indicative of an addiction ..."

"You're spouting off shit," Kyle disagreed. "You're talking out of your ass."

"I'm talking out of my mouth."

"Which is directly attached to your asshole."

Kris laughed and shook his head. "You're an asshole."

"You spit on me," Kyle chided, dabbing the droplet on his forehead.

"I'm leaning back and you're barely facing me, dumbass."

Another drop hit Kyle in the same spot, prompting him to look up at the ceiling. An ominous dark seam slowly spread across the drywall like the shadowy tentacle of a mysterious sea monster. "Um," he whispered, knocking his knee against Kris'.

A loud clanking urged them off the couch just in time for a snowstorm of drywall to pour down on the center of the room.

"What the fuck?" Kris uttered. "Is Matt going to fall through the ceiling?"

"No, you idiot," Kyle replied, craning his neck to get a better view of the damage. "It has to be a busted pipe or something."

"We should call Mom."

"Call her what? A bitch? I agree," Kyle snarked. "What's she going to do about this?"

"Throw money at the problem like she usually does," Kris answered, taking his phone out of his pocket.

"Don't call her. Call a plumber and then text her when it's time to pay him."

"That's way too much work," Kris stated, holding the phone up to his face. "Mom? Yeah, something happened to a pipe under the guest bathroom. Kyle said it probably busted."

"Fuck you," Kyle mouthed, exasperated about what a sellout his twin ended up being. It had taken nearly seventeen years for Kyle to realize what he was dealing with. Kris' loyalty would forever be to a woman who didn't deserve it.

"Yeah, he's here." Kris paused. "For a few days." Another pause. "Because he told me not to." He sighed while Kyle contemplated the best way to murder him. "You can tell him that yourself."

"Tell me what?" Kyle asked, only to be quickly shushed by his brother. "I hate everyone." He theorized what Kris was talking about until his brother inevitably got off the phone. "What was that about?"

"You can talk to her about it."

"Really?" Kyle grunted, aggravated by the blow-off.

"I'm not getting in the middle of this shit," Kris said. "There's no way."

"You're already in the middle."

"No chance," Kris disagreed, shaking his head emphatically.

"What the hell's going on?" Matt questioned, descending the stairs as he wrapped a towel around his waist. "Everything was cool, and then it wasn't."

"A pipe busted," Kyle explained.

"Did you call Mom?" Matt wondered, running his fingers through his wet, dirty blond curls.

"You're a traitor too," Kyle sighed. "I mean, I knew you were, but I didn't think it was this bad. She's going to come over here, and it's going to be both of your faults."

"But the real question is will you still be here?" Kris asked.

"I shouldn't be," Kyle noted introspectively, watching as water sprayed from the pipe. It was inevitable that he'd eventually see Hope, but he had wanted to push the inevitable off for as long as possible. He considered where he could go and decided going anywhere on a Saturday morning was too much effort. Instead, he squatted and dropped his head to his hands.

"The drama," Matt laughed, tussling Kyle's hair.

"The preparation," Kyle replied.

He sat folded in on himself until he heard Hope's voice, and when did, he held his breath.

"What a headache," she groused. "Kyle, go outside and turn off the main shutoff before we flood the place."

Lifting his head, Kyle glared at his mother. "That's your 'hello'?"

Exasperated, Hope pointed at the ceiling. "There's a sense of urgency here, isn't there? The prodigal son returns from his temper tantrum and I'm supposed to ignore the fact that the house is falling apart? Get up and handle the shutoff."

There were a hundred angry words on the tip of his tongue, but Kyle kept his lips pursed tight in an effort not to let them out. In a sense, he understood why she'd delegated the job to him. Now that his dad didn't live with them, he was the only person in the family who actually knew how to handle household tasks. His brothers had never shown interest in the handy things their father had taught them, and it had come easier to Kyle anyway. He missed his dad. It was hard being states away and functioning on separate planes of existence. Kyle didn't want them to grow apart, but how was there a chance of growing together when they lived in different worlds?

As he walked outside, Kyle felt an odd sense of pride. Even after everything that had transpired between them, his mother still relied on him to do a simple thing that his brothers didn't care to figure out. He was needed, and it was comforting. He sighed, aggravated that his heart found a way to get warm over a cold directive. Maybe she would ask him where he'd been and maybe she wouldn't. Regardless, he was the only person in the house who could turn a lever, so that was what he was going to do.

24

Fully enmeshing himself in the business again softened the blow of being back in Hope's house. It seemed his mother had moved on from her concerns regarding his "drug issues" and was content to ignore the problem like she usually did. Of course, with the option of D.C. off the table, it was all Kyle thought about. He spent hours imagining what his life would have been like if he would have gone to live with his Aunt instead of with Mac and Sarah in the motel. Though he'd easily earned back the stolen money, Kyle had yet to forgive himself for his stupidity. He should've known better than to trust them, than to get wrapped up in whatever flirtation had happened between him and Mac. He'd thought his former friend was trustworthy, which had him second-guessing his ability to read people, something he'd believed he was proficient at in the past.

He needed to be away from Tennessee and in a big city. Maybe Washington D.C. wasn't the one for him, but he didn't doubt that he was meant to be in a place where he didn't have to settle for bottom-of-the-barrel "friends" as he did in Iris Valley. As expected, pretty much everybody sucked as much as the backward-ass state did. He couldn't wait to get out and hated that he hadn't taken the opportunity when it was essentially forced on him.

Kyle (4:02pm): I should've let my mom ship me off to D.C.

Richard (4:04pm): D.C.'s further from Texas than Tennessee is.

Kyle (4:04pm): It doesn't matter how far it is. I haven't been back to Texas since we moved anyway.

Richard (4:05pm): You should come for Christmas. I'm sure your Dad would want to see you.

Kyle nodded, though he knew Richard couldn't see him. His dad had told him that he wanted Kyle, Kris, and Matt to come to Texas, especially for Christmas, but it wasn't going to happen. It was ridiculous that custody agreements were arranged without the input of teenage children. Nobody cared where Kyle preferred to be. The document's words were held in higher esteem than his thoughts or feelings. If it were up to Kyle, he would've lived with his father in the first place. It wasn't like Ken was easy on him, but he was leaps and bounds better than Hope. At least he and his father had common interests; there was no bond like that with her. Perhaps that was why it never worked out between Hope and Ken. They were too different. From what Kyle could tell, his parents had tried to make it work. They were married for fifteen years before they called it quits. While there were efforts to stay together for the kids, Hope couldn't stop herself from throwing the marriage away prematurely even though Ken was adamantly opposed to the separation. He didn't want his sons to turn out like the other kids in the neighborhood with divorced parents—pot-head, *losers*. Prior to the dissolution of his marriage, it was common for Ken to rant about kids from broken homes becoming fuck-ups and it had given Kyle a strange sense of security knowing his father felt that way. He'd never thought Hope would actually leave before he and his brothers graduated from high school. He was wrong.

When it came down to it, Hope was too selfish to sacrifice her happiness for the benefit of her children. She had been going through copious amounts of stress after her job loss and felt like Ken didn't love her. The initiation of the divorce was jarringly abrupt and

Hope was very sneaky about it. Ken left town for a business trip and returned to Dallas to two officers greeting him at the airport to serve him divorce papers. From that point on, he wasn't allowed to step foot in the home.

Though it was obvious the spark between them had waned over the years, Ken seemed to have really loved Hope. As far as Kyle was concerned, it wasn't until she lost her job that she became insufferable. Prior to her layoff, she was unavailable, but afterward, she was awful. Kyle doubted that someone could be so psychologically impacted by the loss of a job that it caused them to basically shut down in other aspects of their life, but it had undeniably been a turning point for his mother. The question was if there would ever be a chance for her to turn it around again. He lost more and more hope by the day.

Kyle (4:06pm): He does, but he gets Christmas next year, so it's not going to happen.

Richard (4:06pm): You don't get to pick where you want to go?

Kyle (4:07pm): Nope.

Richard (4:07pm): That's lame.

Kyle (4:07pm): Tell me about it.

Richard (4:08pm): Your mom should lose custody of you guys.

Kyle (4:08pm): Because she sucks or...?

Richard (4:09pm): You ran away to go live in a drug den and she never called the police or filed a missing persons report.

Kyle (4:10pm): You know I would have lost my shit if she did.

Richard (4:10pm): That shouldn't have stopped her.

Kyle (4:10pm): I guess not.

Richard (4:10pm): Did your dad know you were gone?

Kyle (4:11pm): Yeah, but I answered his calls after my narc brothers told him. He knew I was alright.

Richard (4:11pm): Were you alright?

Kyle (4:12pm): I was alright enough.

Richard (4:12pm): And now?

Kyle (4:12pm): I'm still alright enough.

Richard (4:13pm): I guess I'm alright enough with that then.

Kyle (4:13pm): It's all the rage now, being alright enough.

Richard (4:14pm): I feel like we're starting a movement.

Kyle (4:14pm): A revolution of mediocrity!

Richard (4:15pm): I'm in.

Kyle grinned and set his phone down before answering the persistent knocking on the basement door. He swung it open to see Jared standing on the other side. It had been several weeks since he'd been face to face with his former friend. They'd done a good job of avoiding each other in the hallways at school, or at least Kyle did a good job of avoiding Jared on the days he showed up. Kris taking over the majority of the afternoons had helped on the ghosting front too. In hindsight, Jared being repressed or refusing to own his sexuality wasn't the betrayal Kyle thought it was weeks ago. It was interesting how a real act of deception helped to reframe Kyle's picture of past events.

"Wow, you're back," Jared said, staring at Kyle as if he was an apparition.

"You noticed I was gone?" Kyle asked with a smirk. He nodded for Jared to follow him to the couch. "Has Kris been giving you the same hospitality I did?"

Jared laughed. "That's kinda a loaded question, right?"

"Only if your mind's in the gutter," Kyle replied.

"You're a cheeky one," Jared grinned. "If you're asking if he still smokes people up after the purchase, the answer's yes."

"But he skimped on the blowjobs," Kyle tsked, shaking his head with mock disapproval. It was nice to flirt with someone who didn't have a girlfriend hanging off of their jock.

"He lacks the business prowess you have for sure."

Kyle sighed and lit the bong, offering the first hit to Jared. "And here I thought I left things in good hands."

"You have good hands," Jared crooned, blowing the remainder of smoke out of his mouth.

"I do," Kyle agreed, placing one of those good hands on Jared's thigh.

All the aggravation Kyle had felt about Jared melted away as they made out hungrily. Jared may not have been willing to admit to himself that he was gay, but he admitted it to Kyle in his actions. The way he looked at Kyle was gay. The way he touched Kyle was gay. The way he fucked Kyle was gay. And suddenly that was gay enough for Kyle.

With haste, Kyle guided Jared into his bedroom. He wasn't sure if the afternoons were as busy as they had been when they established the business, but if they were, he hoped Jared could get him off quickly. He had a lot of stress to release and knew a good fuck was just what he needed.

"Is this cool?" Jared asked between breathless kisses. "I mean, things got a little weird with us after last time. I wasn't sure if you regretted it or something ..."

"Don't talk," Kyle urged, kissing Jared's voice away.

He didn't need to rehash shit that happened an hour before, let alone a couple of weeks ago. It took too much energy to be relentlessly unforgiving of Hope to take on any other grudges.

Things weren't deep with Jared and Kyle was intent on keeping it that way.

As the make-out session intensified, Kyle's brain left his skull, allowing his body to do what it was created to do without his mind's interference. A month ago, he would have overthought the act and gotten in his own way. His pleasure receptors deserved better and he was going to ensure they got what they sought. Kyle had wasted too much time having expectations of people and getting upset when they inevitably let him down. He'd had expectations that his mother would give a shit and she didn't, that Mac was his friend and he wasn't, and that he could handle pill-popping without becoming a pill popper—no dice. Everything sucked, except fucking, that was always awesome. As far as Kyle was concerned, the only bad sex was sex he wasn't having. So he was glad to be having it, even if it was with someone who may not have been so glad to be having sex with him. There were worse things in the world than being somebody's secret—like being everybody's nothing. He'd dealt with that enough.

25

The day after Kyle decided that expectations weren't worth having, the unexpected happened. It was apropos that the universe would find a way to laugh in his face once he'd finally vowed to keep his head down and mind his own business. He was going to bide his time and make it through the next year and a half at Iris Valley High School in a Xanax-induced haze, not putting effort into anything but homeostasis. He would collect his money from the weed business, not worry about making or keeping friends, and get through the remainder of his high school career in one fucked up piece. It was offensive how circumstances never yielded to intention.

The more school Kyle had missed when he was holed up in the motel, the more popular he'd become. By his second week back after his escapade, he was practically famous—or infamous—around campus. People were intrigued by him. It was as if the drug dealing had whetted their appetite but being enigmatic was like a full meal for the masses. He'd never gotten more attention and had never wanted less. Every smile or "hello" felt as disingenuous as it did suspect. While Kyle had never been a very trusting person, getting screwed by Mac had made him even less so. It was everything he didn't want to think about and exactly what came to mind as soon as someone regarded him in the hallway.

A tap on the shoulder had Kyle turning around, annoyed to be interrupted on his hurried walk to class. "What?" he spat. He shut his mouth abruptly when he saw the handsome face looking down at him.

"It's Kyle, right?" Luke Larson asked, giving Kyle a smile that made his heart race.

"Uh, yeah," Kyle muttered, hating how he clammed up in the presence of muscular men. Luke Larson knew his name. He called him by his name while Kyle stood in awe of him and drooled on his shoes.

"Cool," Luke said. Though Kyle wasn't sure if it was a pause word or a compliment, he liked it.

"What's up?" he asked, as Luke Larson *might* have checked him out. He wanted to sound "cool" because Luke called him "cool," and he figured "what's up" was cool enough.

"I think you're the guy who sells the pot all my buddies smoke."

"Yeah." Kyle's high spirits spun and spiraled to the ground. Luke wasn't interested in talking to him or finding out how "cool" he was. He was looking to score some weed. "That's me."

"Cool, cool," Luke said, with a nod. "How does it work? I usually just smoke my friend's shit, but I think I want to buy some of my own this week."

Not only did Luke say "cool" way too much, he also bummed bud off his friends without buying his own—two highly annoying infractions. Still, Luke being hot as fuck made it easier for Kyle to overlook the fact that his tool-o-meter was registering off the charts. A guy didn't need to be interesting or intelligent when he looked like Luke. He just needed to stand there in all his Greek god glory so mortals like Kyle could stare at him.

"Um, you can come over to my house after school and we'll hook up," Kyle explained.

"Hook up?" Luke smirked.

The heat of a thousand suns burned Kyle's cheeks when he realized his Freudian slip. "I'll hook you up," he corrected, silently considering if there was a possibility that he could evaporate right then and there.

"It's cool," Luke laughed. "I gotcha."

Clearing his throat, Kyle practically croaked, "okay."

There was no doubt in Kyle's mind that Luke Larson thought he was a dimwit. Though the football player was obviously not a skilled orator, he was capable of stringing words together, a skill that Kyle suddenly lacked.

"So, where do you live?"

Kyle handed Luke his BlackBerry. "You can put your number in and I'll text you the address."

Luke raised an eyebrow. "Are you sure you're not just trying to get my digits?"

A hot maelstrom of nausea churned in Kyle's stomach as he stood in the middle of the hallway, exposed. Luke knew he was gay. He could tell by the way Kyle was acting. He was onto him and soon the whole school would know.

"I'm fucking with you," Luke said easily, giving Kyle a companionable smack on the arm before typing his number into Kyle's phone. "You should've seen your face."

Kyle was happy there was no mirror reflecting what he was sure was an unattractive image. He imagined his face was crimson and his eyes were saucers, two features that gave away everything he tried so hard to hide. "I'm glad that I couldn't."

"It was priceless," Luke chuckled.

Kyle didn't laugh along and Luke stopped and cleared his throat.

"Alright, so I guess I'll see you this afternoon."

"Yeah, I'll send the address now so I don't forget," Kyle said, shooting a text off to Luke.

He would've found his own statement funny if he didn't feel so pathetic. The chances of him forgetting the conversation were nonexistent, though he wished he could. He'd spent months daydreaming about what it would be like to actually speak with his crush and the dreams never went nearly as bad as the reality. He wished he could have a redo of the exchange, but he suspected if he did he would still find a way to embarrass himself. All those muscles had him flustered, and he was painfully aware that nobody was ever awed by his presence the way he was by Luke's. While Kyle was convinced that Hope was wrong about everything she ever said, he did wonder if her assessment about his weight was right on. Perhaps if he was bigger, he would instantly get more respect than he garnered as a dainty dude. Kyle wanted there to be a day when he made a skinny guy drop dead just because he was standing in front of him. He hated that every time he came face-to-face with a gorgeous, buff boy, he had the same self-deprecating thoughts. Occasionally, Kyle's attraction to built guys was dwarfed by his craving for the power they held. More often than not, though, he just craved their cocks. It was confusing to want who made him horny while wanting to be them too.

"Cool, man. I'm looking forward to it," Luke said. His smile was as warm as it was satisfied, like he knew how bad Kyle wanted him and liked to have that control over someone.

It sounded like a date. Kyle was sure it wasn't actually date, but it sounded like one. Maybe it was because Luke had never done a drug deal, maybe he didn't understand that it was more transactional than he was making it out to be, or maybe Luke just wanted to make out with Kyle.

"Okay," Kyle said awkwardly, turning to walk away.

He didn't dare to glance over his shoulder as he headed to class. As discreetly as possible, he adjusted the boner pushing eagerly against the seam of his jeans. No matter how much he urged it to calm down, his dick wasn't listening.

"Fuck," Kyle grumbled, walking into the boys' bathroom. He ducked into a stall, unbuttoned his pants, and leaned back against the steel wall. Pulling his cock out of his boxer briefs, he began to slowly stroke himself, picking up his pace as he thought of how Luke's biceps bulged in his leather-sleeved varsity jacket. "Damn," he sighed, closing his eyes as he imagined Luke on top of him, shoving his throbbing cock down Kyle's throat. Kyle would gaze at Luke's big bare chest and abs while the jock treated him like his little bitch boy.

As worked up as he was, it didn't take long for Kyle to get there. Panting and moaning, he shot his release into the toilet. It was only seconds before the shame set in. A jock uttered a few words to him and he was jacking off in the school restroom. It was pathetic. He was pathetic. Tucking himself back into his pants, he pushed his hair out of his face and exited the bathroom.

Dread settled over him as he walked to class. He was late, which wouldn't have bothered him, but he didn't want to get detention and miss out on another chance to act like a dumbass in front of Luke Larson later that afternoon. Though Kyle was sure he was misreading Luke's signals, the slim chance he wasn't had him turned on—again.

"You're late, Kyle," Mr. Stevenson stated, looking perturbed as Kyle entered the room.

"I know. I'm sorry," Kyle replied as genuinely as possible. "I got sick in the bathroom." He noticed a girl in a desk nearby give him a disgusted look and rolled his eyes at her insensitivity.

"You should've gone to the nurse," Mr. Stevenson said. No mercy. "We have rules for a reason and they need to be followed."

"I'm sorry."

Mr. Stevenson sighed. "Well, as you know, I do things by the book, so you'll be serving an after school detention today for your tardiness."

"I was sick," Kyle reminded his teacher. "I couldn't go to the nurse because I was sick and had to go to the bathroom. Should I have vomited on the floor of the hallway?"

"Take a seat."

Kyle did as he was told, wondering who fucking hurt the guy so much to make him such a prick. Taking his phone out of his pocket, Kyle messaged Kris.

Kyle (1:26pm): I have detention today.

Kris (1:29pm): What did you do?

Kyle (1:29pm): I was jerking off in the bathroom, lol.

Kris (1:29pm): You got caught?

Kyle (1:30pm): Sometimes you need a full release, and no, I was late to Stevenson's class.

Kris (1:30pm): He's a fucking prick. Did you wash your hands?

Kyle (1:31pm): Do you want me to lie or tell the truth?

Kris (1:31pm): That's disgusting, bro.

Kyle (1:31pm): Some football player is coming over this afternoon to buy his first bag, so make sure you're there.

Kris (1:32pm): No problem. I love picking up your slack. I've gotten so good at it over the years. Wait is that why you were jerking off? It's ok if you're homo...I'll still love you bro. You can be my wingman.

Kyle (1:32pm): Shut up and be there. I think he's rich.

Kris (1:32pm): I'll take good care of him.

Kyle pouted quietly at his desk. That's what *he* wanted to do.

26

The next morning when Kyle's breakfast was interrupted by the ping of a Facebook friend request, he stupidly thought it was Luke Larson. Though detention kept Kyle from forging a connection, he couldn't get Luke off of his mind. It was different than the way he lusted over him in the past. Luke wasn't a complete stranger anymore. He was a bulked up dude who said "cool" too much, told shitty jokes, and was absolutely perfect. Kyle wanted to know more about Luke, a compulsion that led him to making the mistake of attempting to get information out of Kris. In trying to tiptoe around the point, Kyle somehow insulted Kris and made his twin believe that Kyle didn't think he was capable of handling the business. Every question he'd asked had inspired Kris to become increasingly defensive, therefore more insufferable. They'd fought for the majority of the night, which was fine with Kyle considering it gave him something to do other than daydream about a boy who likely had already forgotten his name.

But maybe he didn't.

Toggling to the request page, Kyle's heart dropped. Sipping his orange juice as he studied the unfamiliar name, he chided himself for thinking it was going to be Luke. Who the fuck was Terrance Brown anyway? While his profile picture looked vaguely familiar, Kyle couldn't place the name. He decided to accept the request though he didn't know his supposed classmate. Maybe Terrance wanted to buy some weed. Kyle wasn't about to turn down some coin.

To Kyle's surprise, Terrance messaged him as soon as they were connected.

Terrance (6:46am): U that guy who sells weed?

Kyle (6:46am): Who wants to know?

Terrance (6:46am): Me. That's why I asked, bitch.

Kyle (6:47am): Bitch?

Terrance (6:47am): Yup

Kyle (6:47am): What's your problem?

"Do you know a guy named Terrance Brown?" Kyle asked Kris and Matt, who shook their heads in unison.

"Why?" Matt asked as he buttered his toast.

"No reason," Kyle replied, staring at his phone as he awaited the asshole's response.

"You wouldn't have asked if there was no reason," Matt pressed. "What's the deal?"

"There's no deal," Kyle said, tentative to tell his brothers what Terrance had typed. He had a nagging suspicion that the guy was somehow linked to Mac and enough had gone down between them that Kyle didn't want to open that can of worms if it was at all avoidable. "He added me on Facebook, and I don't know who he is."

"Who cares who adds who on Facebook?" Kris laughed. "People add people if they like the same band as them. It's dumb. Why are you even trying to figure out who he is?"

"You're too intense in the morning," Kyle admonished, regarding Kris as if he had four heads. "Chill out, dude."

"I'm fucking chill," Kris retorted.

Kyle clicked his tongue. "I know chill, I go to Xanny-land all the time. You're not chill, bro."

"You're right, and I'm not a junkie."

"Junkie," Kyle scoffed, rolling his eyes. "Don't be so dramatic, Kris. It's a prescription drug."

"You lived in a motel for, like, three weeks," Kris reminded, reverting to his new go-to comeback for the sixth time in half as many days.

Too tired to engage, Kyle turned his attention back to his phone screen.

Terrance (6:48am): Ur my problem.

Kyle (6:54am): Yeah, I got that, but why?

Terrance (6:55am): U think u run the game.

Kyle (6:55am): I don't think I run the game. I know I run the game. If I didn't, your punk ass wouldn't be messaging me.

Terrance (6:56am): My punk ass? u got more nerve than u got mass. Thinkin ur so tough cuz ur from dallas...Gonna b a problem 4 u.

Kyle (6:56am): That sounds like a threat.

Terrance (6:56am): not a threat, a promise.

Kyle (6:57am): You're right I am from Dallas and I'd call this representin' bitch!

Terrance (6:57am): U will see.

Perplexed by the aggression, Kyle gnawed on his lower lip and debated telling his brothers what was going on. The guy was probably all bark and no bite, some feral Tennessee dog who never learned not to piss on things he wanted to claim.

"What's wrong with you?" Kris asked, gently kicking Kyle's leg under the table. "You look like someone just told you your dog died."

Or that a rabid dog was going to kill him. "I'm fine," Kyle decided in an effort to reassure himself and his brother. He got up to put his cereal bowl in the sink and grab his jacket. "I'm walking today."

"Walking?" Matt questioned. "It's cold out."

"That's why I have a coat," Kyle uttered as he bundled himself in his winter gear.

"Why would you walk when you can ride in a warm car?" Matt pressed. "It doesn't make any sense."

"Kyle doesn't make any sense," Kris stated matter-of-factly. "You can't try to make sense of the nonsensical, so don't even try."

"You're cranky," Kyle tsked.

"I'm not cranky. I'm just saying stuff you don't want to hear," Kris asserted, "and it's my duty as your twin to make sure my voice is in your head as much as yours is."

Kyle laughed and shook his head. "You're crazy."

"I make good choices, and you make bad ones. I'm the angel on the devil's shoulder."

"No offense," Matt interjected, "but you make a ton of bad decisions too, Kris. You're far from an angel. The idea that you'd be Kyle's guiding light is ridiculous."

It wasn't often that Kyle was glad to hear from Matt, but he had to appreciate that he was dragging Kris.

"Name two bad decisions I've made in the last two months," Kris demanded, glaring at Matt who didn't seem fazed by the anger in his brother's eyes.

Deciding that he didn't want to witness the culmination of the epic fight that was brewing between them, Kyle left the house and headed toward school. He shouldn't have been shaken up by the messages from Terrance. He was probably just a wannabe dealer who was aggravated that Kyle had the lion's share of the market. When you were on top, there were always people who wanted to tear you down. Terrance was most likely one of them, hungry for the success Kyle had achieved.

As he walked to IVHS, Kyle focused on his morning ritualand fished a pill and a twenty-dollar bill out of his pocket. He felt the tension in his body melt away as the Xanax went up his nose, feeling a sense of complete relaxation. He spent the rest of his walk daydreaming about Luke while anxiety about Terrance slowly dissipated.

By the time he arrived at school, Kyle was horny as hell and hoping to run into the football player. While he would have been thrilled to have a chance to have a more coherent conversation with Luke, Kyle would settle for watching him from afar and collecting more spank bank material. Goddamn, he was hot.

As Kyle took off his coat to hang it in his locker, he felt a crushing blow to the back of his head. The pain radiated as he instinctively raised his hand to check for blood.

"Told you it was a promise, bitch," the voice behind him growled.

Swinging around just in time to catch the next swing of Terrance's fist, Kyle clutched his aching jawline. "Holy shit. What's your fucking problem?"

He'd never been in a real fight before. Growing up, skirmishes with his brothers were the norm but they'd never gotten to the point where Kyle was concerned he'd be left with long-term effects. The sound of girls shrieking reverberated in his ears as another punch sent him crumbling to the ground. He did his best to protect his skull from the boot that seemed intent on bashing it in.

A chorus of "stop" and "get off of him" filled the hallway as a swift kick to his stomach robbed Kyle of every ounce of air he'd had in his lungs. He braced himself for more abuse, but instead of another wave of pain, he felt strong hands tucked under his armpits, lifting him to his feet while a teacher restrained Terrance.

"Are you okay?" a guy he didn't recognize asked as Kyle lifted the bottom of his shirt to wipe the warm stream of blood off his face.

"I don't know," Kyle admitted, too dizzy to stand up straight. He leaned back against the lockers, hoping the room stopped spinning soon.

"Sorry, man," the stranger said, patting Kyle's arm companionably. "It seems like you pissed that guy off pretty good."

"Yeah, I guess so," Kyle replied, glancing at the crowd gathered in the hallway. Among the sea of mostly amused faces was Luke Larson's. His Knight in Shining Armor from the dream he had months earlier was standing with a group of guys, playfully reenacting what Kyle assumed was the attack. A churning in his belly led instantly to Kyle vomiting on the slick white tiles and a collective groan of repulsion from the onlookers. Luke didn't give a shit about him—nobody did.

"Somebody should help him," a girl said, "he's so small, and that guy went in on him hard."

To add insult to injury, it was two cheerleaders who came to his aid, flanking him on either side as they held his elbows and lead him to the girls' bathroom.

"What did you do to that guy?" the blonde cheerleader asked, wetting a paper towel so she could use it to carefully dab blood off of Kyle's chin.

"I don't know," Kyle answered honestly as he allowed himself to be taken care of by the random bystander. He knew people went crazy when their money was messed with, but there was no way Terrance was a real player in the game when Kyle had never heard of him until that morning.

"Are you sure you didn't steal his girlfriend or something?" the brunette asked, giving him a sympathetic smile. "That seemed like a 'you-took-my-woman' beat down."

"I'm sure," Kyle promised, wincing as the blonde moved the paper up to his wound.

"I'm sorry," she muttered, concentrating on her task. "For this and for what happened."

"It's not a big deal," he said, attempting to play off the event even though in reality he found it quite devastating.

"Nobody deserves that," the brunette asserted. "Guys are assholes sometimes."

"A lot of the time," the blonde added.

"I'm a guy," Kyle replied, grimacing when the grin he tried to give them split his injured lip. "Fuck."

"Shh," the dabber hushed, going back to work. "You're making it worse."

He didn't tell her that was typical for him.

27

Kyle wasn't sure why he felt the need to reach out to his mother after the altercation with Terrance, but he did. Deciding not to fight the compulsion, he took a seat in his first period class and texted Hope.

Kyle (8:04am): Can you pick me up? I just got in a fight.

Mom (8:06am): A fist fight?

Kyle (8:06): Some guy sucker punched me in the hallway and beat the shit out of me.

Mom (8:06am): Are you kidding?!

Kyle (8:07am): No joke.

Mom (8:07am): Are you okay?

Kyle (8:07am): I'm ok, but I want to leave. I'm tired and everyone in class is

bugging me about the fight.

Mom (8:08am): I'll pick you up.

Kyle (8:08am): They won't let me leave. Can you come in and tell them I've got

a doctor's appointment or something?

Mom (8:08am): And what about him? Did the school resource officer arrest him?

Kyle (8:09am): No. He went to his next class, I think...walked

Mom (8:10am): Unbelievable!

Kyle (8:10am): Yeah.

Mom (8:11am): I'm coming to get you.

Kyle (8:11am): Don't make a big deal about it, ok? It's not a big deal. I'm just tired.

Mom (8:12am): Unacceptable!

Kyle (8:12am): Really, it's not a big deal.

But it was. That's why he'd told her, because it was a big deal and he wanted his mom to intervene. Hope was a very intelligent and powerful woman, especially when provoked—a total ball-buster. Secretly Kyle wanted her to go to work making everyone's lives as miserable as his was.

Mom (8:13am): Someone ATTACKED you and you're telling me to ignore it?

Kyle refrained from telling her that that was what she usually did. Hope was fired up, and it felt kind of ... good.

Not even ten minutes after the last text message, the classroom phone rang. Kyle watched his teacher nod and glance in his direction.

"Kyle, you're needed in the principal's office," his teacher informed him, practically shooing him toward the door.

Kyle's classmates appeared to be invested in his exit, which was laughable considering they weren't interested in intervening when he was getting kicked in the stomach a half hour before.

Upon his arrival at the office, Kyle was ushered directly into the principal's office—a strange V.I.P. service he wasn't prepared for. He wondered how brutal Hope's berating was to earn him the special treatment. Taking a seat in the chair across from Principal Smith's desk, Kyle smoothed the thighs of his jeans nervously. Though he was used to meeting with administration in West Lake when he was nothing more than a boisterous student, he wasn't accustomed to being in the principal's office in Iris Valley. It was funny that he caused more trouble in Tennessee than he'd ever dreamed of in Texas, yet he still flew under the radar at Iris Valley High School. It made him wonder if the staff was overwhelmed by kids worse than Kyle or if they were so tuned out that they didn't care.

"We received a call from your mother claiming that you were assaulted in the hallway this morning," Principal Smith began.

"I was."

"Well, we take accusations of assault very seriously at Iris Valley High. If you were, in fact, assaulted, we will throw the book at your assailant."

"I guess that's good to hear," Kyle replied, clearing his throat as he adjusted uncomfortably in the chair. There was no denying his body was sore, and he was sure it would only get worse in the coming days.

"Do you have his name?" the principal asked.

Kyle had heard that snitches got stitches and all the other gangster mantras, but he had no reason to protect a sucker-punching piece of shit. "Terrance Brown."

"Got it. He'll be disciplined," Principal Smith nodded, writing the name down in a notebook on his desk. "Now that that business is out of the way, how does your mother know about

the fight? She's already called us."

"What? I texted her from class," Kyle huffed, incredibly confused by the question.

"As you know, the use of personal phones on campus is strictly prohibited. You shouldn't be using your cell phone in class."

"Are you serious?" Kyle questioned, flabbergasted by the turn of events. "I figured this was an extenuating circumstance."

"We prefer to make those determinations," Principal Smith stated brusquely. "Students typically believe their judgments will align with the school's and that isn't the case."

"Some thug beat me up. There shouldn't be any debate over appropriate phone usage right now."

"And there isn't," the principal assured Kyle. "You'll face the ramifications of breaking the rules as anyone else with an infraction would. You need to turn your phone in and pay the ten-dollar fee to get it back tomorrow."

"Seriously?"

Principal Smith nodded his confirmation. He had no idea what he was in for. Hope had spent the better part of her corporate career squashing smug sycophants. She'd prided herself on standing up for what was right rather than what was widely accepted in the company. Kyle wondered if that position had something to do with her eventual layoff. Either way, Kyle knew

Principal Smith was in for a Hope scolding that matched or superseded the one he had no doubt already received that morning. Kyle had never been convinced that Hope cared about him, but he knew she certainly cared about being right. If Principal Smith thought he was going to spout off a bunch of bullshit rules and not experience the wrath of Hope Ross, he had another thing coming.

Kyle handed over the phone and muttered: "I'll be getting that back soon."

"What?" Principal Smith asked.

"I think she should be here soon."

"You can wait in the sitting area until your mother arrives," Principal Smith said.

Following the directive, Kyle left Principal Smith's office and sat on a chair in the lobby. The way the secretaries regarded him told Kyle that they were privy to what had happened. He didn't appreciate the pity in their eyes. The last thing he needed was to be a victim, even though that was exactly what Terrance Brown had made him.

He wasn't sure if he should have been mortified or proud of his mother's vehemence. As a kid, it always embarrassed him when Hope got involved with any of his activities. She was brutal to coaches and teachers who crossed her children. In hindsight, it was more about the power than the protection, but Kyle didn't know it at the time.

When Hope came barreling into the office with steam billowing out of her ears, Kyle knew that anyone in her path was in for it.

"Let me look at you," she demanded, dropping to her knees in front of Kyle so she could study his face. "Your lip's busted." Her fingertip moved slowly up his bruised cheek to his orbital bone. "And you're definitely going to have quite the shiner. This kid did a number on you."

"I'm fine," Kyle said, hearing the slight warbling in his voice. As if the emotion welling in his chest wasn't indication enough that he may cry, the stinging in his eyes acted as a pathetic confirmation. He wasn't going to let one tear loose, not in front of the secretaries or his mother.

"You're not fine," Hope disagreed. "Nobody who's attacked in a place that's supposed to be safe is *fine*." She pushed Kyle's hair out of his face and told him: "It's okay not to be fine, Kyle. You don't always have to say you're alright when you're not."

Too close to the edge, Kyle didn't dare say a word. Instead, he nodded his understanding and prayed Hope got out of his space. His mother should have been the person in the world he felt the most comfortable crying in front of. After all, she was the one to hold him the first time he ever cried, but she wasn't that person—not even close.

"The principal took my phone." Kyle finally uttered.

"What? Why?"

"Because I texted you about the fight from the classroom. He said I need to pay to get it back

tomorrow".

Standing up and placing her hands on her hips in a Wonder Woman stance, Hope stared down the administrative assistant. "Where's Principal Smith?"

"I'll give him a ring and see if he's available to talk," she answered, quickly lifting the receiver as she kept a nervous eye on Hope.

"See if he's available," Hope scoffed with a sardonic laugh. "He better be available. I got off the phone with him ten minutes ago and told him I was on my way."

"Um, I'm checking," the older woman promised. "I'm sure it won't be a problem." She turned her attention to the call. "Yes, Principal Smith, Mrs. Ross is here to see you."

"Ms.," Hope corrected.

"Ms. Ross," the secretary said sheepishly. "Okay. Thank you." She hung up the phone and addressed Hope. "He'll be coming up to take you back to his office in a moment."

"We'll be here," Hope snapped, turning to Kyle. "Do you want to wait in the car, baby?"

"Are you serious right now?" Kyle questioned, unable to hold back his laughter. "Baby?"

Hope narrowed her eyes at Kyle, unamused by his amusement. He wondered how his mother kept a straight face during her little charade. They were in an intense stare-down when Principal Smith walked into the room.

"Mrs. Ross," he greeted, approaching Hope with his hand outstretched.

"Ms. Ross," she grumbled, obviously perturbed that she had to make the same correction to both the secretary and the principal.

"I'm sorry. Ms. Ross," he nodded. "Come on back. He gestured for Hope to walk with him and Kyle begrudgingly followed.

"Are you wobbly on your feet, son?" Hope whispered, loud enough for the principal to hear.

"No," Kyle answered flatly, thinking it was definitely a mistake to have involved his mother.

"Please take a seat," the principal said once they reached his office. He waited for Hope to sit before he did. "Now, first and foremost, we apologize to you and Kyle for the incident that occurred on campus. No student should feel unsafe in our halls."

Kyle lifted an aching eyebrow. Damn, Smith was full of shit. The difference in his demeanor in front of Hope was marked. Kyle doubted he would bring up the phone infraction to his mother. It wouldn't be in his best interest, yet ...

"We do have one additional issue to discuss," Principal Smith stated, as Kyle sat in shock that the guy was actually going to poke the bear with his asinine assertion of the rules. "Kyle contacted you after the assault through use of his cell phone. We have very strict phone usage policies here at Iris Valley High School ..."

"Before you go any further," Hope interrupted, her pointer finger held up as if she'd made a discovery. "Are you implying that Kyle's use of a cell phone to contact me after he was attacked was somehow inappropriate?"

"I'm saying—" Principal Smith began. He was quickly cut off by Hope telling him exactly what he was saying.

"You're saying that somehow my son was in the wrong to reach out to his *mother* after he was savagely beaten in *your* building. You'd better rethink that."

"I'm just ..." the administrator stuttered, obviously shocked when Hope jumped out of her seat.

"We're done here," she stated, waving for Kyle to stand up. "This is ludicrous. Until you're ready to focus on the problem at hand, we can't have a productive discussion."

"I assure you we can focus on the issue at hand," Principal Smith said quickly. He was out of his chair and moving toward the door at the same pace as Hope. Kyle almost expected to see him block the exit. It was a strange exchange, and one he wanted over as soon as possible—by whatever means necessary.

"I don't feel well," Kyle muttered, effectively drawing his mother's attention.

"What's wrong?" Hope asked placing her palm on his cheek. "Sore?"

Kyle nodded and Hope adjusted the purse on her shoulder. "This discussion isn't over," she told Principal Smith. "Well, the part about the phone is over. That was dead before you broached it. We'll discuss the attack when my son is feeling better. I want him coherent for his testimonial."

"Testimonial?" Kyle repeated, confused. He rolled his lips in tight when Hope shushed him.

She gave him a curt nod. "That's right. We have a lot to discuss."

Principal Smith looked as anxious as Kyle felt.

Hope had that effect on people.

28

It was a relief for Kyle that Christmas break was only a few days after the assault. Though he tried to act like he was unaffected by the incident, it wasn't true. His Xanax habit and the fact that Terrance Brown was suspended couldn't alleviate the stress the attack had caused. It was exhausting to constantly look over his shoulder, expecting another blindside. There would be no reason for anyone to go after him, but he hadn't thought there was a reason before and Terrance had found one.

Surprisingly, the situation had brought Hope back to the house. Instead of sporadically showing up for breakfasts, she actually spent several nights at a time in her own bed. Kris and Matt wanted to believe she was present to be supportive, but Kyle doubted it. He figured that she and Jimmy had reached the stage in their relationship where they looked forward to doing their own thing. Either way, she was bad for business. If there was one thing her lack of family time was good for, it was running a pharmacy out of the basement. The holidays had their clientele stressed, and Kris and Kyle could only do so much to move the product right under their mother's nose. It was odd that she was suddenly invested, yet still so out of touch.

The many more hours she spent at home were dedicated to

talking about how disappointed she was in Iris Valley High School. It was crazy to Kyle that she had expected so much more of a high school in the middle of Bumblefuck, Nowhere. He'd always thought she was in tune with the way shit worked—or didn't—but it seemed she wasn't as with it as he'd believed she was. It was disheartening to get to know his parents as he grew older. He assumed it was the same for other kids. Everything he thought he knew about them was the version they wanted to sell. It was when he realized they were human —and not the superheroes he'd believed them to be—that his reverence for them had started to wane. It couldn't have been easy to be charged with the responsibility of three wild boys, but the army of nannies Hope had hired made managing them seem impossible. Little had Kyle known at the time that his mother had struggled to handle her own life.

By the time school was back in session in early January, Hope had made the decision that it would be their final semester at IVHS. Matt was unfazed, considering he was on track to graduate, but Kris and Kyle were skeptical.

"What do you mean we're done here?" Kyle asked as he pushed the meatloaf she'd prepared for dinner around on his plate. It was strange enough that Hope had cooked something other than soup beans and even more shocking that she was saying exactly what he'd wished she would for months.

"This semester will be your last at Iris Valley High," she repeated, regarding Kyle as if he were a simpleton. "How is that difficult to understand?"

It was a loaded question. Hope had never been fickle—or overly concerned—so her sudden intensity was perplexing.

"There's no other school around here," Kris pointed out, glancing at Kyle. Kyle knew the look. His twin was as confused as he was.

"There's a lot to figure out, but you won't be attending that school anymore," she said, letting out an exasperated sigh. Kyle thought she was caught in her feelings, but her next statement assured him that people could only come so far. "You need to eat your dinner, Kyle. Don't you think for one minute that that boy didn't target you because you were an easy mark. Bullies don't sucker punch guys with muscles. They look for the weakest and meekest."

"Yeah but that just shows how weak they are," Matt interjected. "Like, there's no glory in dominating a little skinny wimp." He turned to Kyle. "No offense. I'm a skinny wimp, too."

"Not as skinny as Kyle," Hope asserted. "He's a twig."

"He's still sitting here minding his business," Kyle reminded them, frustrated that his body remained a hot topic of conversation in the Ross house.

"Eating his dinner," Kris added, gesturing at Kyle's plate.

"Not enough of it," Hope admonished, shaking her head in disappointment. "This is why I never cook. It's not worth it."

"Oh, that's why?" Kyle asked sarcastically, earning a glare from his mother. "You always

overcook the meat anyway. It tastes like dog food. Maybe I would've been bigger if you had actually cooked good food for me as a kid. Now I have a lot of catching up to do, and I can't stomach your food."

Wordlessly, Hope stood up, grabbed Kyle's plate, walked to the trash can, and tossed the entire thing into the bin.

"You threw the plate away!" Matt exclaimed, his eyes wide at the scene.

Hope didn't reply, instead she left the room without looking back.

"She's crazy," Kyle uttered.

"You were rude," Kris replied. "She spent a lot of time cooking this afternoon, and Lord knows she's awful, but you were rude."

"I was rude?" Kyle cried. "As usual, she was picking on me and giving me shit about my weight. I mean, she said that I wouldn't have gotten my ass beat if I was bigger. That's serious victim blaming and it's fucked up."

"She always talks that way," Kris said matter-of-factly. "You'd think you would be used to it by now."

"Why should I have to be used to it?"

"That's a good point," Matt chimed in. "And it did sound like she was blaming him for the attack."

"I never said it didn't," Kris groaned. "I'm just saying why go there with her?"

Kyle rolled his eyes. "Hope Ross' constant defender. Her knight in shining armor over here."

"No. I'm just not cutthroat like you are."

"You're both annoying," Matt stated, reaching for another helping of mashed potatoes.

"Honestly, I'm sick of listening to all of you."

"So plug your ears, asshole," Kris snarked.

"Yeah, tune us out," Kyle grunted.

As usual they were back together, quick to shoot Matt down and find some common ground.

"Focus on Mom, okay?" Matt sighed. "Leave me out of it."

"You put yourself in it," Kris retorted.

Finished with the conversation, Kyle grabbed a beer out of the refrigerator and headed down to his bedroom. As usual, Hope had completely shit on the good news simply by being herself. He wanted to know what she was planning for them regarding school and if the change she referenced meant another move.

Though he knew his father was generally out of the loop, Kyle figured he was the best bet for finding out major life-changing information.

Kyle (7:18pm): Hey Dad

Dad (7:19pm): Hey there. How are you?

Kyle (7:19pm): Alright. How about you?

Dad (7:20pm): Great.

Kyle (7:20pm): Have you talked to Mom recently?

Dad (7:21pm): She called me the other night.

Kyle (7:21pm): About what?

Dad (7:21pm): Stress with the apartment building.

Kyle (7:21pm): Oh. That's it?

Hope constantly had issues with her investments. After losing her job, she'd cashed out her individual retirement account and bought several apartments in West Lake. It should have been a sign that she wasn't going to go back to work, but they'd thought she was only diversifying.

Dad (7:22pm): Yup. Tenants aren't paying. She mentioned having to spend more time on the grounds, making them aware that their rent was due on the first of the month and that she'd be there to collect it.

Kyle (7:24pm): I'd pay her to keep her away.

Dad (7:24pm): Me too. I got lucky.

Kyle (7:24pm): You made out like a bandit. Can I get a divorce from mom too?

Kyle (7:25pm): Did she mention anything about me and Kris going to a different school next year?

Dad (7:25pm): Vaguely.

Kyle (7:25pm): And what did she say?

Dad (7:26pm): No details.

Kyle (7:26pm): Why's she so shady?

Dad (7:26pm): I try not to think about it. I was going to call you tomorrow to share some exciting news.

Kyle (7:27pm): Do tell.

Dad (7:28pm): The Ross family reunion is officially scheduled for the weekend of March 14th in St. Louis.

Kyle (7:28pm): at Uncle Jerry's?

Dad (7:28pm): Yes. I'll work out your flights this weekend and send you guys the confirmation when they're booked.

Kyle (7:29pm): Awesome.

Dad (7:29pm): It will be a great time.

Kyle (7:29pm): I'm excited. It gives me something to look forward to.

Dad (7:30pm): Life in Tennessee isn't doing it for you?

Kyle (7:30pm): Don't even get me started.

Dad (7:31pm): I was under the impression things were getting better.

Kyle (7:31pm): Where'd you get that from?

Dad (7:32pm): You haven't been beaten up or run away to a motel in a while.

Kyle (7:32pm): I love how that's the new threshold.

Dad (7:33pm): The boondocks are crazy.

Kyle (7:33pm): She's crazy for wanting to live here.

Dad (7:34pm): You'll learn one day that she's crazy for a lot of reasons.

Kyle (7:35pm): I've been feeling that way for a while now.

Dad (7:35pm): She's still your mother.

Kyle (7:36pm): Yeah, thanks a lot for that.

Dad (7:36pm): You wouldn't be here without her.

Kyle (7:37pm): In Tennessee?

Dad (7:37pm): On Earth.

Kyle (7:38pm): Oh. Either way, thanks for nothing Hope!

Dad (7:38pm): Get excited for St. Louis.

Kyle (7:38pm): I am.

Dad (7:39pm): We'll have a blast.

Kyle (7:39pm): I know we will.

That was one thing Kyle never doubted. The Ross family knew how to entertain, and they didn't spare any expense. Unlike Hope's side of the family, Ken's was wealthy and happy to spend on merriment. While others would dread the announcement of a family reunion, thinking it would be full of boring games and nosy aunts prying into love lives, for Kyle it was the promise of a much-needed break from his mom and Tennessee. He couldn't wait to get away from them both. March couldn't come soon enough.

29

The more someone looked forward to something, the longer it took for the awaited event to arrive. At least that was Kyle's experience. He never considered himself an impatient person, but the high level of anticipation he experienced in the weeks leading up to the Ross family reunion had him thinking otherwise. Days turned to years the closer it got to the trip and Kyle was fiending for a release. Even Xanax didn't have the power to calm him in the way that looking forward to getting out of Iris Valley did. The moment he boarded the plane to St. Louis, Kyle breathed a sigh of relief.

Though Hope never expounded on the statement she had made weeks earlier about changing schools, it was apparent in the way she regarded IVHS that her vendetta wasn't going to be easily assuaged. For once, Hope's ability to hold a grudge was an asset for Kyle. He needed her to stay angry enough to pull the trigger and get them the fuck out of the hellhole they were rotting in. Every time Hope made an off the cuff comment deglamorizing the state she had unrealistically gassed up in their inaugural months, Kyle became further convinced that they would be gone by summer. He tried not to get his hopes up, because his Hope was a consistent letdown, but it was nearly impossible to quell the excitement. He could taste the escape.

And in St. Louis, freedom was the tang of perfectly balanced deviled eggs, meticulously

crafted hors d'oeuvres, and a never-ending array of cream based "salads." It was too bad that Hope wasn't around to see him scarfing down the amazing offerings at the family reunion. His commitment to tasting everything and going back for seconds would have been considered admirable by his mother. Still, he was thrilled that she wasn't around. Hope's absence gave Kyle a chance to let loose in a way he couldn't when there was the threat she'd show up.

"Do they not feed you in Tennessee?" Uncle Jerry teased, taking a seat next to Kyle at one of the long banquet tables set up in the older man's expansive backyard.

"Not anything that tastes as good as this," Kyle grinned. "Aunt Lilly is a great cook."

Jerry nodded proudly. "She sure is. That's why I married her. Well, that and her bedroom behavior." He laughed heartily at Kyle's repulsed expression. "What? You're seventeen. I'm sure you know all about the birds and the bees by now."

"Knowing about the birds and the bees and Aunt Lilly's 'bedroom behavior' are two different things," Kyle replied, sure his cheeks were bright red.

"Your Dad told me you had a hot little girlfriend."

"I did," Kyle confirmed. "We broke up a while ago."

"That's too bad," Jerry said, sympathetically patting Kyle on the back.

"Eh. It wasn't a big deal," Kyle replied easily, taking a sip of his Bud Light.

Jerry raised his eyebrows. "Is that right? Do you have another one lined up?"

"I wouldn't say that..."

"It's good to play the field at your age," Jerry asserted. "You've always been a smart boy."

Kyle smiled at his uncle. He'd take the compliments wherever he could get them. "Thanks."

"Are you going to join in on the fun or continue to eat your weight in macaroni salad?" Jerry asked, gesturing toward the grassy expanse where family members were playing games like croquet and horseshoes.

"I'll play soon," Kyle promised. "But for now I have more damage to do."

"Oh to be a teenager again," Jerry said wistfully, patting his beer gut. "I don't know where you put it all."

"Right down my throat," Kyle smirked.

Jerry chuckled, clapped Kyle on the back, and got up from the table.

The thought of shoving things down his throat had Kyle reflecting on how long it had been since he'd had a hookup. Deciding the drought needed to end, he took his phone out of his pocket and downloaded the app he'd been too much of a pussy to keep on his phone before. There was no need to spend time making his profile shiny or complicated. Instead, he uploaded a shirtless picture that he'd sent to Jared previously and marked his age as eighteen. It was easy to reel a guy in.

It took mere moments for Kyle to receive a message.

MrChristianGay (8:03pm): Hey Cutie.

Kyle toggled to the guy's profile. He was forty-six years old, had rock hard abs, a big dick, and a sexy silver fox vibe. Kyle was game.

Kyle (8:06pm): Hey. What's up. I'm Kyle.

MrChristianGay (8:07pm): Nice to meet you babe, I'm Christian.

Kyle (8:08pm): Hey Christian. Any plans tonight?

MrChristianGay (8:09pm): I was getting ready to hit a few clubs with my friends, but now I'm

looking to do something else. I'd love to take you to dinner.

Kyle (8:09pm): That's not necessary.

MrChristianGay (8:10pm): I'd love to eat that ass.

Kyle (8:11pm): That's more like it. Except I don't have a car.

MrChristianGay (8:12pm): You're in Chesterfield right now?

Kyle (8:12pm): Yeah. I'm here for a family reunion. I can try and sneak away. Can you pick

me up in 15 minutes and drop me at the Hilton later?

MrChristianGay (8:13pm): Text me the address and I'll pick you up.

Kyle (8:14pm): I'm at the corner of Maple and Frontier.

MrChristianGay (8:14pm): Sounds good. I'll head that way soon.

Kyle (8:15pm): Okay. What are you driving?

MrChristianGay (8:15pm): Black Hummer.

Kyle felt his dick stiffen. He was eager for a hot military dad to fuck him

around for the night. What a sexy car. He couldn't wait to ride in it and then on Mr. Christian Gay. Shoving his phone into his pocket, he crossed the yard to where Kris was playing croquet with their younger cousins.

"You want in?" Kris asked, glancing up.

"No thanks. I have somewhere to be. I'll be back at the hotel around midnight," Kyle said, figuring three-and-a-half hours was ample time to get his rocks off.

He was wrong. Mr. Christian Gay turned him out and then rewound it and did it all again. Kyle had never been fucked like that in his life and he was happy as hell that he'd taken the chance to meet up with the dynamo. There was something to being with an older man. Christian knew exactly what he was doing, and thankfully Kyle got to benefit from his years of experience. On top of the physical pleasure, Christian made Kyle feel awesome about himself. Never before had Kyle been with someone who was into his body the way Christian was. It was empowering to have someone show attraction to his slender frame instead of making quips about it.

"You're the perfect little twink. Do you know that?" Christian asked, tracing his fingertips up the slight curves of Kyle's straight body.

"Isn't that, like, a derogatory term?" Kyle laughed, tucking his face into his lover's toned bicep.

"If it is, it shouldn't be. It's cute, like you."

Kyle hummed happily and nuzzled his nose against Christian's warm skin. "You think I'm cute?"

"Beyond cute. Perfect," he stated, raking his fingers through Kyle's hair. It was soothing.

"I'm telling you, you have the type of body men worship."

Kyle propped himself up on his elbows to stare at Christian, shocked by the statement. "Which men? I've been around a lot of them and believe me—they're not worshipping me."

"You've been around *boys*. Boys don't know how to treat a man like you. They only know how to be boys."

Kyle chuckled as Christian leaned down to give him a kiss. He could get used to the praise. He hadn't realized how hungry he was for it until the need was fulfilled.

"Guys like you are rare," Christian continued. "Small but strong as hell. It's a major turn-on." Christian proved his statement by pushing his hard cock against Kyle's thigh.

"Damn." Kyle grinned as Christian looped his arms around his waist and pulled Kyle on top of his built body.

As he climbed back on the older man's dick, Kyle was convinced that he could be what Christian had said he was: small but strong and worthy of feeling good about the body he'd spent much of his life getting criticized for. It was amazing what the needy hands of a grown-ass man could do for his self-concept. Though it was a random hookup, Kyle felt something shift within him in that stranger's house. He wanted that kind of attention—positive, praiseful attention.

When Christian finally drove Kyle back to the hotel at three in the morning, Kyle was shocked to see several police cars in the valet circle.

"Shit," he muttered, as he recognized his father, brothers, and uncle Jerry standing in the middle of the brouhaha. Kyle sunk lower in his seat as they drew closer, trying to avoid their searching eyes. "Pull around to the back entry," he directed, garnering a confused look from Christian.

"You're eighteen, right?" he asked.

Kyle could see the realization dawn on the older man's face. "Yeah," Kyle lied, but he knew Christian didn't believe him.

Without another word, Christian stopped the car at the rear door and stared ahead at the dumpsters in his vision line.

"Uh thanks," Kyle muttered, not daring to give the statue a goodbye kiss.

Climbing out of the car, Kyle hurried into the hotel, fiddling with his wallet to free the room key as he raced down the hallway. The faint sound of police sirens in the distance had his heart pounding in his chest. Slinking into the room, he plugged his charger into his dead phone and got into bed as if he'd been there for hours. A few minutes after the screen of his phone illuminated a small section of the dark room, the entire space was flooded with bright lights.

"Where the fuck have you been?" Ken roared, stomping over to Kyle's bedside.

"Huh?" Kyle asked sleepily, determined to play it off. "Here."

"Bullshit," Kris spat. "We checked up here every ten minutes for the last two hours."

Matt didn't say a word, moving through the motions of his bedtime routine.

"Where were you?" Ken pressed. The devastation in his eyes told Kyle that his father knew exactly where he was.

"Nowhere," Kyle answered vaguely, wishing he would have stayed at Christian's place and dealt with the consequences in the morning.

"Your friend said otherwise to the search team we called upon when you disappeared three hours ago," Ken grunted. "I can't believe you."

"A search team?" Kyle asked. "I wasn't even gone for a night."

"The start of one," Kris amended. "St. Louis isn't known for being a safe city, idiot."

"Who was he?" Ken demanded. "The guy you were with. He said he dropped you off after a 'hookup.' What does that mean? Was he selling you drugs?"

"It means they had sex," Matt said quietly. "Like I told you downstairs."

Ken shook his head as if he couldn't fathom the possibility. "There has to be a different explanation."

"Would it be more desirable if I was buying drugs? Chilling in some crack den?" Kyle inquired, the swell of vomit rising in his throat. He never imagined the moment he came out to his family to be as combative as it was. He never imagined it at all.

"Kyle," Ken gasped. "What are you trying to say?"

"I'm not saying anything," Kyle decided, terrified to venture a glance toward his twin brother. "I'm going to bed."

"And that's it?" Kris asked. "No other explanation?"

Kyle didn't reply, burying his face in his pillow to stifle his whimpers.

His brothers and father were silent as they got into their respective beds. The lack of conversation was deafening and Kyle wished someone would say something, even if it was something he didn't want to hear.

Finally, after approximately twenty minutes of excruciating quiet, Kris whispered from beside Kyle, "I think he got arrested."

Kyle didn't reply. It was awful to think that his lie could impact Christian's life. They had both been looking for the same thing and what they'd found instead was heartache and exposure. In the end, it wasn't as good of a night as it had appeared to be hours before. As usual, something that had seemed amazing in the moment would be forever sullied by the memories that followed it. And everything was a mess.

30

After the revelation about his sexuality, Kyle had expected to wake up to a shit storm of anger, and it was a bit alarming when he didn't. Though Kyle felt like everything was different, it was business as usual for his brothers and father. It would have been less jarring if they would have at least acknowledged what had gone down. The way they purposefully ignored the situation bothered Kyle more than a berating would have. On one hand, it was a relief to not have to hear what they thought of him, but on the other, their silence spoke volumes. Kyle didn't want to be regarded differently because of his preferences, but he did want to be looked at rather than looked over.

It was a month before anybody brought up the topic of his orientation again.

"So you fuck guys then?" Kris asked Kyle bluntly as they sat in their typical spots on the basement couch.

The question took Kyle aback and rendered him speechless for a moment. It would have been easy to lash out, start a fight and shut down the conversation with a tantrum, but Kyle was too emotionally exhausted to play games. He'd waited for weeks for someone to say something, *anything*. He wanted the conversation over with.

"Yup," Kyle replied, taking the joint from Kris' fingers.

"Yup?"

"Did you expect me to say no?"

"I don't know," Kris admitted, looking perplexed by Kyle's response. "Do you like it?"

"Yup," Kyle answered plainly, drumming his fingers on his thigh.

For a beat, they sat in a less comfortable quiet than they were used to. Even during their worst fights, there was never a feeling of detachment. Kyle hoped that they were connected too closely to be torn apart.

"We're identical twins," Kris stated, pummeling the quiet that had concerned Kyle.

"And ...?"

"And I'm not into fucking dudes."

Kyle raised an eyebrow. "Do you know that from experience?"

Kris crinkled his nose and shook his head, peeved by the question. "No."

"Well then how do you know?" Kyle asked, garnering another expression of disgust from his brother.

"Ew. I could never. Fuck, I can't even think about it."

"Then don't," Kyle suggested, rolling his eyes at Kris' dramatics.

"But we're made the same—DNA, everything. How can you be gay if I'm straight?" Kris wondered, taking a hit from the pipe.

"Maybe the universe has a sense of humor?" Kyle offered, taking the bowl from his twin's hand.

"Are you going to marry a guy one day?"

Kyle choked on smoke at the inquiry, sputtering as he tried to find the right words. He settled on, "I don't know."

"How do you not know?" Kris pressed, furrowing his brow in skepticism or confusion.

"I don't think about getting married," Kyle replied, matter-of-factly. "Do you?"

"Not really."

"So ..." Kyle held up his hands for affect.

"Fair point."

There was another stretch of silence, but it was more comfortable than the previous one.

"Does Mom know?" Kyle asked, nausea churning his stomach as he considered the next level of exposure.

"I didn't tell her, and I doubt Dad did either."

"What about Matt?"

"He wouldn't." Kris paused. "You really don't want her to know, huh?"

"She's a big enough bitch to begin with, I don't need to give her any more ammunition than she already has."

"I was going to ask if you really thought she'd give you a hard time, but she definitely would," Kris relented. "In her eyes, it would be one more thing you did to make your life difficult."

"Yeah, so there's that."

"That there is," Kris agreed, nodding his head. He rolled his lips in tight, as if he was struggling to cage the words that wanted to come out of his mouth.

"What?" Kyle prompted, relatively nervous about what was to come.

"Am I still allowed to call you a faggot? I mean, now that you are one. Is that offensive?" Kris asked, serious as can be.

Kyle laughed at his brother's intensity. "Nah. You're the fag anyway."

"You literally suck dick," Kris exclaimed, immediately getting shushed by Kyle who was too aware that Hope was upstairs in the kitchen, no doubt making something disgusting for dinner. Kris lowered his voice. "How am I the fag?"

Kyle shrugged. "I'm not sure, but you manage to be. It's not about being gay. It's about being a pussy-ass bitch like you are."

"So you're redefining the word 'faggot' now?" Kris chuckled.

"We've been doing that for a while. Everyone has been. It lost its meaning years ago."

"And you're the expert?

"You just made me the expert," Kyle smirked.

"Do you feel qualified for that position?"

"Fuck no."

"Was that guy who kicked your ass your boyfriend or something?"

"What?" Kyle cried. "Not even close."

"I thought maybe you broke up with him and he was pissed or something."

"You're ridiculous," Kyle chided. "He was pissed that we have the whole market and that's it. It was about money, like everything else."

"Why didn't he come after me then?" Kris asked skeptically.

"It's not hard to see that I'm the brains of the operation. I guess he figured if he took out the nucleus, the whole cell would be destroyed."

"The nucleus?" Kris guffawed. "You think pretty highly about yourself."

Kyle would have objected, but in that one area of his life, he did. He knew he was business-savvy and their wallets confirmed his prowess. Kris always reminded Kyle that they would've made more money if they had remained in the Xanax trade, but Kyle didn't care. Xanax kept him calm while weed kept him rich. It was an equilibrium of sorts, and as far as Kyle was concerned, it was working.

When spring sprang and Hope finally informed Kyle and his brothers of her plan to move back to West Lake at the end of the school year, Kyle was surprised at how torn he felt about the news. He'd spent nearly a year hating everything about Iris Valley and dreaming of the day he would get the fuck out, but as soon as he heard that they were heading back home, he was concerned. It wasn't a penetrating worry that bore its way through his Xanax shield, but it was present nonetheless. There was no way they would have been able to pull in the cash they did in Tennessee while in Texas. The monetary success had allowed Kyle to grow accustomed to a certain sense of freedom he had lacked when he lived in West Lake. He could buy whatever he wanted without asking his parents for assistance, and when a good chunk of his purchases was drug-related, Kyle appreciated the autonomy.

He shouldn't have been concerned. He should have been over the moon, and he hated himself for being torn. Would he ever be truly happy if he always wanted what he couldn't have?

"So are we getting a new house in West Lake?" Matt asked. "How does this all work?"

"We'll be moving back into our house," Hope answered, shifting uncomfortably on the basement sofa. "How do you boys sit down here all the time? It's horribly lumpy."

"Yeah our landlord's brutal," Kyle replied.

"Landlord? Since when are you paying rent?" Hope shot back.

"Touché," Kris laughed, earning an unimpressed glare from Kyle.

Turncoat.

"So how are we moving back into our house when you sold it?" Matt asked, undeterred by the tangent the conversation had taken.

"I never sold it," Hope stated as if it wasn't a huge bomb to drop.

"You said we couldn't afford it anymore," Kyle reminded her. "That was the main reason why we moved to Iris Valley."

"I never said that," she denied, shaking her head fervently.

"You most certainly did," Matt asserted. "That was the impetus for the whole move."

"Says who?" Hope questioned.

Kyle laughed sardonically. "Are you kidding? That was your big story less than a year ago. You promised the move wasn't about your loser boyfriend and was because we couldn't afford to live in Texas."

"How would that be the case if we still have the house? Hmm?" Hope asked, strategically ignoring the fact that they never knew she was able to hold onto the house.

"You're so full of shit," Kyle cried, unable to handle the frustration she was causing him for another moment.

As he stormed into his room, he heard Hope ranting about how he was impossible to please. She was right. Her lying mouth would never be able to please him, even when it was delivering good news. Wondering how deep the betrayal ran, Kyle texted his father.

Kyle (4:57pm): Did you know Mom still had our house in West Lake?

Dad (5:02pm): In case you didn't notice, I'm out of the loop with just about everything.

Kyle knew it was a dig at him and he decided rather than engage, he would abort the mission and move on to communicating with some who wouldn't give him shit.

Kyle (5:05pm): Guess who's moving back to Texas?

Richard (5:06pm): I feel like there's only one correct answer to this. Hang on, let me think about it for a minute. I want to get it right.

Kyle (5:07pm): Stop messing around and say something nice.

Richard (5:07pm): My dreams are coming true.

Kyle (5:08pm): That's more like it.

Richard (5:08pm): Seriously. This is great news. When will you be back?

Kyle (5:09pm): A few weeks. After Matt graduates.

Richard (5:10pm): Where are y'all going to be living?

Kyle (5:10pm): Oh get this, Hope never sold our house.

Richard (5:11pm): Come again? I thought that was why y'all were moving in the first place...because she couldn't afford to keep the house anymore.

Kyle (5:12pm): She claims she never said that.

Richard (5:12pm): Of course she does. If that isn't typical Hope behavior, I don't know what is.

Kyle (5:13pm): You make me feel less crazy.

Richard (5:13pm): Well, that's a good thing considering you're moving back home. I can do it on the regular. Lord knows you need it.

Kyle (5:14pm): I need something.

Richard (5:14pm): You must be happy.

Kyle (5:15pm): I am, but I'm aggravated.

Richard (5:15pm): And that's typical Kyle behavior.

Kyle (5:15pm): What's typical Richard behavior?

Richard (5:16pm): OCD and self-loathing.

Kyle (5:16pm): We're quite the crew.

Richard (5:17pm): Back together again soon.

Kyle (5:17pm): Hell yeah.

Texas Forever.

31

It turned out that the transition back to Texas wasn't as seamless as Kyle thought it would be. While he'd been stalled in Tennessee, everything back home had moved full speed ahead. His group of friends didn't embrace him the way he expected. At first, they were happy to see him, and then it was business as usual, with everyone focusing on their own shit rather than worrying about making sure Kyle and Kris felt reassimilated. There were no questions about Tennessee or debriefings regarding what they'd missed. They were just *there* instead of being a point of focus. Kyle had always looked forward to the summer, but he found himself anticipating the school year even more. School would bring structure. He would have classes with his friends and wouldn't have to worry about who was hanging out with whom and which event he wasn't invited to. The summer was one big confirmation that he had a horrible fear of missing out. When he was in Tennessee, he didn't worry about being excluded from things, because he was excluded from *everything*. It was more stressful being in close proximity to his friends and knowing that he didn't always get included. He could only rely on Richard's company so much.

To cope with the litany of changes he hadn't expected, Kyle

doubled up on his usual dose of Xanax. The more numb he was, the less he thought about how horribly Hope had fucked up his life. The initial move had started a snowball effect, and the only way to weather the relentless blizzard was to pack his nose full of powder. Everything would have been so simple if Hope wasn't so damn complicated.

In an effort to shift his concentration away from the world he no longer fit into, Kyle focused on what he'd grown to know. The only reason Kris and Kyle had gotten into dealing drugs was to have the money to get out of Tennessee when they turned eighteen. Since they had escaped the Volunteer State by their seventeenth birthday, Kris had tried to convince Kyle that they should retire from the business and focus on having fun during their senior year at West Lake High School. Kyle wasn't hearing it. There was no way he was going to ignore the opportunity to make some serious cash. Their hometown was an upper-class suburb where money was tossed easily from peoples' hands. He wanted a piece of that action and the immense distraction it would provide.

Getting the business off the ground proved to be a difficult process. Kyle had grown so used to not having Hope around all the time that he forgot what it was like when she was. Even at her most present in Tennessee, she wasn't in the house nearly as much as she was in West Lake. That, coupled with the less private living quarters, made setting up shop in their home significantly more challenging.

As if the issue of location wasn't bad enough, dealers in Dallas were a dime a dozen. Many of them were selling dozens of dime bags for prices Kyle couldn't match and still make a profit. In Iris Valley they had the market cornered, but that was far from the case in Texas. He couldn't find a supplier who didn't laugh in his face when he pitched them their cut. His last meeting was the one that solidified the fact that he needed to abandon his hopes of making it in the Dallas market.

"You're not in Kansas anymore," an older dealer snarked as Kyle exited his apartment late one night.

"Tennessee," Kyle corrected, wondering why he mentioned the state to begin with.

"There's no fucking difference," the guy chortled. "You ain't there. That's all I'm saying. Leave the business to the big dogs around here, Toto, or you're gonna get bit."

The thought of more Terrance Browns coming out of the woodwork to take him out was enough to steer him away from the possible riches.

"I don't know what to do without the cash flow," Kyle complained, tossing an apple in the air as he lay on the living room couch watching Kris and Matt play video games. "I spoiled myself."

"You do realize you didn't do it all on your own, don't you?" Kris asked, aggressively jabbing the controller with his thumb. "I'm sick of you talking about how awesome you were when I was right there beside you the whole time."

"You took over for a while too," Matt reminded Kris, who nodded emphatically.

"I sure did. If anything you were a leech on the business," Kris asserted, dodging the apple Kyle launched at his head. "Asshole. Don't get salty with me when I bring up facts you don't want to acknowledge. Honestly, I'm glad the whole thing died. You became a liability."

"You're delusional," Kyle admonished.

"You are," Kris disagreed. "It's probably a side effect of all the Xanax you snort. Delusions of grandeur."

"I doubt it," Matt said, garnering a glare from both of his brothers. "I could look it up if you don't believe me." He paused the game and began fiddling with his phone.

Kyle thought about going in on the dingbat, but decided that wasn't worth commenting. He was happy to let Matt busy himself out of the conversation.

"How was I a liability?" Kyle persisted. "It was *my* money we used to start the business.

You couldn't have done it without me. I paid for it all and then made sale after sale after sale after sale ..."

"Okay, okay," Kris hushed, "I get the point. I've told you a hundred times and I'll tell you a hundred more—you put most of our potential profits up your beak."

"That's what you don't get," Kyle began, sitting up as he prepared to go into battle. "You can't count money you didn't make as a potential profit. The only profit is one that's accounted for. I could come up with tons of ways we could've made more money, but we didn't do any of them so they wouldn't be our 'potential profits.'"

"But we were working on selling Xanax and then we had to stop because you were hoarding it all. We knew how much we stood to make if we would have continued selling it," Kris retorted.

"Xanax doesn't cause delusions of grandeur," Matt interjected. "See, I told you."

Kyle and Kris ignored their brother as they continued to have the fight they had at least three times a week. They should have been exhausted from making the same arguments, but they were just as vehement as ever.

"I don't even think it's the money you miss," Kris stated. "I think the business gave you a sense of purpose that you can't grasp now."

"Since when did you become a psychologist?" Kyle scoffed.

"He's pretty good," Matt complimented, garnering a grin from Kris.

"Thanks, man."

Matt shrugged. "It's true."

"I think you're wrong," Kyle said, ignoring the brotherly lovefest he wasn't a part of. "It's definitely about the money."

"Bullshit," Kris asserted. "It helped your self-worth. You felt like a big man for the first time in your life. Power like that is intoxicating."

"It sounds like you're talking about yourself."

"Not quite. I'm happily willing to let it all go. You're the one who's trying to hold on even though it's clear that it's done and over with now that we're back home."

Kyle rolled his eyes, not wanting to hear the possible truths his twin was sharing. "Whatever."

"It's easy to brush it off and act like I'm completely off-base. It's harder to actually reflect on the shit I'm saying and consider the chance that I might be right," Kris said, hitting the pause button so he and Matt could get back to their game.

Matt glanced over his shoulder at Kyle. "For the record, I think he's right."

"Yeah, I gathered that," Kyle replied. "You better pay attention, or you're going to get your ass beat."

"Is that a threat?" Matt bristled.

"No, dummy. I meant in the game," he answered, gesturing toward the television.

"Ah."

"Why should today be different than any other day?" Kris smirked.

"Honestly, something happened to you guys in utero that made you into egotistical monsters," Matt sighed. "It's like a birth defect that I avoided because I was in there a year before."

"Don't talk about mom's vagina like it was some kind of luxury hotel," Kyle shuddered.

"First of all, it was her uterus. Babies don't grow in the vagina, imbecile," Matt tsked. "Second, that thing housed three babies within the course of twenty months. That's the Ritz Carlton of uteruses."

"I'm going to puke," Kyle grumbled, lying back down. "I don't want to hear about mom's innards."

"The word 'innards' is grosser than anything Matt just said," Kris declared. "Who says innards?"

"Who calls a vag the Ritz?" Kyle shot back.

"The uterus," Matt corrected.

"I swear I get stupider hanging out with you guys," Kyle muttered, pulling a pillow onto his face in an attempt to drown out their voices.

Though Kyle would never admit it aloud, the things Kris said about his worth being tied to the business had given him something to think about. It was a tough pill to swallow and one that he wasn't sure he was willing to open up for. He didn't think of himself as weak, but Kris' assertions made him feel that he could be. There was so much for Kyle to be self-conscious about, and his capability to do well in entrepreneurial ventures alleviated some of that internal stress. Was it so wrong to find value in things he was good at? Maybe the skills weren't necessarily mainstream marketable, but they could transfer eventually. Either way, he wasn't going to feel guilty about mourning something that was important and meaningful to him. One day he had it, and the next day it was gone. It was devastating and similar to a suffering he'd experienced second-hand.

Kyle closed his eyes, though his face was hidden by the pillow. The realization was powerful enough to bring tears to his waterline.

It was Hope's story, too.

EPILOGUE

It took Kyle a week to come to terms with the epiphany he had while lying on the living room couch. How did he not see it clearly before? How his life ran parallel to his mother's in so many ways. How he fell into many of the same patterns she did. How the things he hated about her were things he did himself. He wondered if the stress of the years to come would wear on him the way it had worn on Hope. If one day he would give up because it was easier than failing and if his acquired apathy would ramp up and make it difficult for him to maintain relationships with the people who were supposed to matter the most to him. Eventually he wouldn't need Xanax to check out. His mind would be in defense mode and automatically shift a switch to stop caring. He'd move across the country for a man who made him feel good about himself and leave once the confidence didn't stick. He would chase the feeling because the majority of the praise he'd earned otherwise was eradicated with his job.

It was so easy to imagine disappointing his own family one day. He'd disappointed his parents and brothers so easily over the years. His children would fault him for all of his faults because they would be born expecting more and getting less. He had a hard time giving affection. He'd tell them how successful he used to be, as if the world had turned its back on him rather than him forgetting he had to adapt to the world. He'd make himself the victim and admonish others for doing the same thing. Every choice he made would be based on opportunity and the chance to exert the minimal amount of effort. He'd be a winner who lost once and lost the will to win again.

The fear he experienced every time his brain took him down the same panicky path washed over him as he sat on the dock of his dad's lake house. The sun's warmth kissing his skin couldn't assuage the chills that moved through his bones. He needed to worry less about complaining and more about figuring out another way to make it. There had to be more than one route to success. He wasn't going to be like Hope and let one defeat be his kill-shot.

Perhaps Hope had always known that Kyle was a lot like her. Maybe that's why she was harder on him, because she was aware he needed to be toughened up to be stronger than her. Despite a growing understanding of Hope's possible motivations, he'd never forgive her for her callous approach. There had to be better ways to teach a kid to be strong that didn't include constantly telling him how weak he was. Kyle was the visual representation of everything Hope feared: someone too wafer-thin to stand firm against the wind.

Lying flat on the splintery wood slats, Kyle gazed up at the big Texas sky, freedom that could only be reached by his eyes. He would never get away as long as he was bound by his mistakes. There was no escaping himself, no matter where he tried to run. For so long, Kyle had

masked his anxiety by taking a pill, and in doing so, he could barely remember much about Tennessee. He'd lost a year of earned memories, even if they were crappy ones.

It was a lesson his mother had never learned, and one Kyle was committed to facing head-on. He had to be better than her, and the only way to rise up was to be bigger and tougher than she'd ever been.

A twink—small but strong. Perhaps that was who he was, a sinewy soul dealing with a decline in Hope. Maybe that's who she made him. His mother had always hated his body, but Kyle was determined to love it, if only to spite her. He rolled his back muscles into the surface below him, acknowledging that his spine was made of steel and his limbs of iron. No matter how soft he looked from the outside, people didn't know the strength he held within his skin. It was odd to lie baking under the rural Texas rays and feel his body slowly come alive. He'd felt disconnected from himself for too long, and there were no more excuses. He was home.

And he was going to be okay.

THE RISE UP SERIES

Book Three

February 2019

CPSIA information can be obtained
at www.ICGtesting.com
Printed in the USA
LVHW030236311018
595214LV00005B/554/P

9 781732 322523